Together We Rise

22.3.25.

Together We Rise

ISBN: 9798302953797

www.richiebilling.com

For those who fight for freedom, justice and equality

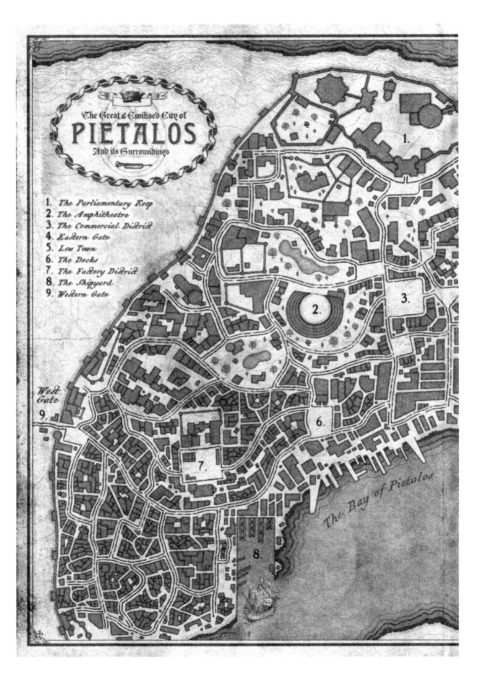

The Great & Civilised City of

PIETALOS

And its Surroundings

1. The Parliamentary Keep
2. The Amphitheatre
3. The Commercial District
4. Eastern Gate
5. Low Town
6. The Docks
7. The Factory District
8. The Shipyard
9. Western Gate

West
Gate
9.

1.

2.

3.

6.

7.

8.

The Bay of Pietalos

The Copper Cliffs

4. East Gate

5. Tewbrucke

THE GREAT RIVER

About The Soundtrack

For this book, I wanted to do something different. Music has always played a massive role in my writing. It can inspire me, stir emotions, and spur me to keep going when I feel like giving up.

Music has the power to add a whole new dimension to a story. More often than not we experience the wonderful effects of music and scores in film and TV. I wanted to bring that to a book. With the help of a tool called Udio, I've been able to do just that.

As you move through the story, you will see at the beginning of each chapter a musical note and a QR code. Scan the code and you can listen to the song on YouTube.

Each character has their own theme song, and it reflects the emotional journey that they go on in that chapter. The idea, I hope, is to bring you closer to the story and to help feel what the characters are experiencing.

I hope you enjoy this extra dimension!

Richie

Revolution Begins Within

The Healer

There was a chance, a slim one, that this morning would be the last in an era of misery and despair, that tomorrow a new sun would rise on the beleaguered people of Pietalos. Dhijs clung to that hope as he made his way through the streets, careful not to disturb the precious pre-dawn quiet. Seagulls glided through the blue spring sky, their squawking muted. Even those nesting on the crumbling apartment blocks and tenements were quiet.

Dhijs found his eyes drawn to the red letters printed on a government poster plastered against one of those tenement walls. "Uproot The Root" it read. Below the text was a crude drawing of a man stabbing another man to death, a pipe and pile of root dust beside him. Dhijs sighed. This was a new one, not that the previous shock-and-awe posters had done anything to stop people from smoking root. He shook his head and caught his reflection in the window next to the poster. His grey beard was long now. He often kept it trimmed short, if not shaven clean. His patients were not as receptive when he had a beard—they seemed to distrust his advice, and that made him feel like a snake oil salesman.

Dhijs's thin and straight white hair was too long as well. Today he had it fastened back in a tail. Bertha would never have let him look so unkempt. She would have sheared him like a sheep before letting him leave the house. Always thinking of others first, that was her way. Even when she was sick and on death's door, she asked about neighbours and friends, how they were doing, whether they needed anything. Being unable to save her nearly broke him. He tried everything. She worsened until one day her breathing grew shallow and she slipped away. And with her went the precarious confidence he had in his ability to help people.

Grief callouses with time and things change, but if Bertha saw him now, years on, she'd still recognise the faded red cloak that hung over his shoulders, which remained a staple of his appearance. "Doctor Tomato" a toothless woman had called him once. Not a name he liked. A young lad had called him the "Red Wizard" many moons ago. He liked that better. If nobody could agree on a name for Dhijs, they could at least agree on the role he performed in society—he healed the sick and injured, or at least tried.

But as much as Bertha would have scolded him for his shabbiness, things like his appearance didn't matter to him anymore. All aspects of his life had become unimportant, bar one. And today, he would learn whether all the planning, all the pain, all the hardship was worth it. An internal voice whispered that it was a waste of time, the task impossible, that too many would die. *No. It will always be worth it, no matter the outcome. To fight for what you believe in, to stand up for what's right, is always worth it.*

Dhijs walked on, eyes on the masts of the merchant ships that crept into view as he climbed the hill. Once, the Bay of Pietalos swelled with ships. Nowadays, even the most innumerate of people could count them. He followed the road as it wound down toward the bay. Weed-infested tenements with hole-ridden roofs lined the road. The smell of rotting wood and filth was pungent even outside. Yet people still called these places home. In the doorway of one building, he saw the moon-like eyes of root addicts looking out at him. Honest working people, just looking to get by, emerged from other doors. And among them lived the petty criminals, the pushers and the prostitutes, growing in number as the spreading destitution swallowed up whoever it could sink its claws into.

2

A sound stopped Dhijs in his tracks—the shrill call of a magpie. He looked up and found a single black and white bird perched upon the roof of a tenement. Dhijs saluted it, an instinctive reaction. His mother had done it often when he was a kid, and he'd copied it ever since. *And here I am, sixty years on.* The bird took off into the mist, heading toward the bobbing masts.

Life buzzed like a beehive at the docks, and this morning was no exception. Fishermen who had worked through the night brought in their haul—and it grew more meagre every season. It was unloaded by warehousemen and stevedores who hauled boxes and crates and loaded them onto carts pulled by mules and oxen. The docks never slept, just like the waters they depended on. With so many people working here and carrying out dangerous jobs, there were plenty of injuries to tend to. And more often than not, bodies for the undertakers to recover and bury. Dhijs ventured down here each day and had done so for the past who knew how many years. From cuts and gashes to missing fingers and crushed limbs, there was always something waiting for him.

The merchants and ship owners used to pay him to treat their wounded staff. That had stopped some time ago, along with other investments in the wellbeing of the people. They were deemed the lucky ones for having a job, not the employers for having staff who gave a damn. The injured paid their own way now, if they could—some owned nothing more than the rags they wore. Dhijs would never turn his back on the needy for a lack of coin, though. Those he did help often paid him back in kind—with food, pilfered supplies, information, the odd favour. He always valued those types of transactions more than any coin with a dead monarch's face on it.

Outside of his first stop, the fish market, he saw a crowd gathering. They huddled around a man standing on a box. He had a long beard with shells and pinecones dangling from it, fastened with bits of twine, and shaggy brown hair and a heavy cloak of faded blue that enveloped all but his bare, grubby feet. Dhijs knew him well—Cytion, once a carpenter of mixed repute and now something of a preacher and town crier.

"All of our futures are at stake!" he shrieked, turning heads and drawing more attention. "Is that what you want? To allow evil hands to guide you to your doom? For it is evil at work, for how could anyone with a shred of humanity conjure a place so cruel and wicked as Pietalos? It is a place of nightmares, and we are all silently complicit. That is, until we break the shackles and take back our futures." A few people clapped.

Dhijs remembered a time when Cytion stood alone in squares and on busy corners discussing the failings of the republic, how it was as corrupt as the fallen monarchy, how the lives of everyone in the city and country beyond, the working man in particular, were being manipulated, controlled, and destroyed. There were theories about election rigging too, and schemes to kill people so the rich-born could profit. Crackpot Cytion, they called him. Dhijs once saw a woman splatter an egg on his head and a group of kids pelt him with cat shit after a speech on what he saw as a dire need to stop dumping sewage in the Great River. But in the past few months, Cytion had, at last, found an audience with his attack lines on the government, on increases in taxation, on the rising price of food and lack of clean water. And that audience was growing. Even now, at dawn on a dreary morning, he had listeners looking for answers, even from a man who looked as trustworthy as the "instant-cure" medicine men who rolled into town from time to time. And they ought to listen too, for Cytion was right—for the most part. The government *was* corrupt and broken. Something needed to change, and more and more people had begun not just to realise it, but to demand it.

"Healer, do you agree?" Cytion called out as Dhijs walked by. His audience turned to him. Many of them were young, men and women both, frustration palpable in their dark-ringed eyes. There was hunger there, too, for something more than stale bread; for change, to feel some sense of hope that they had a future worth living for.

"Agree with what?" Dhijs replied.

"That taxes should be distributed for the benefit of all and not hoarded by the elite or spent on an army we don't need."

"Yes. Completely."

"And what of this, my friend, do you think that those taxes should be used to pay for good doctors like yourself to treat the sick and injured, to care for the frail?"

"If there is money there to spend, then what finer way to do so than to put an arm around your fellow man and tell him that everything is going to be okay. What impact do you think that would have on the heart and soul of that person, to help them through their worst and most troubling of times? I'll tell you. They would feel something greater than a loyalty to city or country. They would feel part of a society that cared. And that can help shape who we are as people, what we stand for in life, what we want our world to be like."

Cytion clapped his hands and hopped up and down on his crate, cackling with laughter. "Here, my friends, is a learned man." He bowed to Dhijs. "I bid you the finest of days, my friend."

"And what a fine day it will be," Dhijs said, nodding to him and the crowd before heading toward the market. He'd wanted to say more. Perhaps he'd even said too much. More than a few times these past weeks, he'd almost let slip something he shouldn't have. It was excitement, nervousness, and a hearty dose of apprehension. He knew the possibilities of what today could bring but also the horrors of what would happen if it went wrong.

He entered the fish market—a square with a tin roof, open on all sides. At one time, you could find fish of every kind here, from long-legged monsters hauled up from the depths of the Sea of Dragons to the shimmering trout that called the Great River home. The city's demand for fish, which it sold at a premium to their neighbouring countries, had destroyed the delicate cycle of life. Fishermen now went further out to sea in order to scrape a living, some in small crafts not built for waves so big and powerful. Too many didn't return. Even larger boats had been sold, with fishermen laid off. Fewer fish meant fewer jobs in the market and processing factories that had sprouted up along the river bank as well. That wasn't to mention the food shortages in the city of half a million people. The pursuit of profit had pushed them all to the precipice.

Dhijs moved through the counters lining the market's many walkways, trying not to look at the dead fish upon the tables. He'd never been one for fish—he was born far from the coast. It was the smell he disliked, but he'd grown used to it. Breathing through the mouth helped. He headed to a quieter part of the market hall where the wounded fisherfolk gathered. Not many awaited his care today. One giant of a man with a crooked nose had a deep gash across his hand after he tried to grab onto a fishing line. Dhijs cleaned and stitched it and sent him on his way. A young lad, pale as flour, had lost a fingernail, a nasty wound, and he was visibly struggling with the pain and stress of it. No doubt his first painful injury on the job. *It won't be the last, I'll wager.* The rest were a mix of cuts, strains and sprains, all mild.

Washing his hands after finishing up with his last patient, Dhijs heard pained cries over the bustle of the market. They grew louder, and they were heading in his direction. Into the tiny room burst two men, a small man with a pinched, weasly face. The other man was tall with midnight-black hair and skin to match. He had an arm around his little companion. His other arm was tucked close to his stomach, wrapped in a rag that was stained crimson.

"Lie down on the table," Dhijs said. The wounded man trembled as he did so, tears of pain streaking his cheeks. "What's your name?"

"Luki," his companion answered for him.

"Not so much today," Dhijs said, giving his warmest smile to try and change the mood. "What happened?"

"We was unloading barrels and casks from the ship, rolling them up from the hold for the crane to take 'em. We had to secure 'em with a rope, but as it was lifting one, it snapped and fell as Luki was rolling another barrel into place. The fucker damn near crushed every bone in his hand," the little man said, his accent thick yet rhythmic.

Luki groaned.

"Not every bone, I'm sure," Dhijs said.

"Doc, you shoulda heard it."

Dhijs shot him a look. The little man took the hint and shut up.

Dhijs unravelled the rag and found that Luki's friend was right—a catastrophic crush. Bursting with blood, bone, and ligaments; a complete mess. He didn't know how Luki was still conscious. The poor bastard's lips were trembling now. Dhijs checked his pulse, and the temperature of his forehead and the back of his neck. His eyes were unfocused, sweat lining his brow.

"Luki, can you follow me okay?" He nodded. "Unless you know some kind of miracle-working surgeon in this gods-forsaken country, your hand is fucked. If you want to live, you've got one choice—it's going to have to come off. Leave it as is, it'll get infected, and that'll kill you within a week or two."

"No," he said, and for a moment his eyes focused. He sat up, made to move, but a gentle hand from Dhijs kept him still. "I can't lose it. I can't. What would I do? I won't be able to work. I can't earn. What about the kids? The missus? They'll fuckin' starve."

"You got anyone who can help you? Family? Friends?"

"Nah. Not in this town. Everyone's already on their arse. Who's got the time and spare coin to help a cripple?" He grimaced, eyes bunching with pain. Tears ran down his cheeks.

"There's always a way, even in a system as broken and crooked as ours. But you won't have a future if you don't let me take off this hand. It can't be fixed, and you're losing too much blood."

"You might as well let me go, Doc. What prick is gonna hire a cripple? And what kinda work could I even do? All I've ever known is that warehouse, and look what happens when the job fucks me. They blame me for it happening and kick me out the door."

Dhijs sighed, looked down at the poor young bastard. He used the cleaver more often than he liked in this job. Every week someone suffered an injury like Luki's. And it all could be avoided if companies stopped treating their workers like disposable commodities. Each time he used the cleaver, he tolerated doing it less and less. But in many cases, amputating a limb, hand, or foot was the difference between life and death. As Luki said, though, life as a cripple was hard in their uncaring city. If something stopped someone from getting by, that was it. Discarded. Deemed invaluable, as if human beings had one function—to work. The government offered no safety net, no help. That was why so many permanently injured people went one of two ways—trying to make coin by committing crimes, or trying to forget their woes by smoking as much root as they could, or whatever mind-numbing substance was available. It created a vicious cycle that even the most well-intentioned of people struggled to escape from. But it was possible, and it still might be for Luki.

"I can see it now, Doc, what the rest of my life will be," Luki said through gritted teeth. "It happened to my uncle. He lost half his foot working in a forge, couldn't walk proper, couldn't earn any cash, and ended up on the root. Smoked it every day till his body couldn't take no more."

"Well, you're mighty fine at chatting shite, so I think you're worth keeping around for that. I'm going to give you something that'll knock you out and deaden the pain," Dhijs said.

Luki began to weep, but he didn't object to Dhijs's plan. His "friend" had slunk away without a word.

"Doc, what if I don't wake? That's it. That's the end." Dhijs could see fear in his eyes as the nothingness yawned before Luki. Dhijs saw it often in those he treated. Those who despaired often didn't make it.

"Look at me. This is not the end. I'll look after you." He placed a reassuring hand on his shoulder. Luki looked down at Dhijs's hand, then up into his eyes. He took a deep breath.

"Drink this," Dhijs said, handing Luki a phial.

"Smells like piss."

"You guessed the secret ingredient right." Luki drank with a grimace. "Look at me now, Luki. Focus. Remember this. When you're able, come and find me here. I'll see that you and your family aren't forgotten."

Luki nodded, eyes closing, and then he was off. Dhijs set a metal poker to heat in the heart of the brazier, boiled some more water, and took out the cleaver from his bag.

After cleaning up and leaving Luki to sleep off his poppy milk, Dhijs found himself ravenous. He grabbed a salt cod sandwich—the one type of fish he could stand to eat—and went off to find a quiet spot. Cytion was gone, no doubt having moved on to a busier spot now the rest of the city had awakened.

Dhijs was glad to find his usual perch on a low stone wall vacant. He loved the view of the bowl-shaped Bay of Pietalos, and here it was free of both people and ravenous gulls. Though he spent his days helping others, he sometimes found people exhausting. Seated, he unwrapped the paper covering his sandwich and took a hearty bite into the thick brown bread. The warm fish flaked in his mouth, breadcrumbs decorating his beard. His gaze drifted across the harbour to the men hauling sacks and loading wagons, directing hoists and bellowing orders. Scores of starlings gathered around the fishwives, hoping for scraps. The gulls spread their great wings to scare them off. More of them circled above in a blue sky that was losing ground to dark rain clouds. With a flash of black and white, a magpie swooped by, landing upon the rusted tin roof of the fish market. It flicked its tail and cackled. A heartbeat later, two more landed beside it. They called and were answered by another magpie perched on the mast of a nearby ship. The rhyme his mother sang when he was a child played over in his head...

One for rain,
Two for sun,
Three foretells a tremendous gain,

And four of a life just begun.
Five means your deeds will end in vain,
And six heralds heartache and pain.
Seven foretells treachery, terrible and sly.
Eight or more means the end will soon be nigh.

Dhijs had asked her what the words meant and where the poem came from, but she hadn't known. Seeing four magpies boded well, though. A good omen for today, though he wasn't the most superstitious of people. He often wondered about the meaning of things, the purpose of it all. He was certain life wasn't meant to be so miserable. Tomorrow, he hoped, would usher in the first day of a new path.

After brushing the crumbs from his lap, he looked up, and there she was. Those captivating green eyes, round and dominant in her waif-pale face, looked at him with amusement. Her hair, black as a raven, was tied back in a ponytail save for a strand that hung over her right eye. It added to her luminous complexion.

"Good morning," she said in her soft and delicate voice before taking a seat on the wall beside him.

"You're nervous," he said.

She looked at him, eyes narrowing. "How can you tell?"

"I can see it in your eyes."

She smiled. "You read me better than I know myself. Scarily so. How do you see these things so well?"

"Look at the body, the face, the eyes. How do they carry their shoulders? Where do their eyes wander when they speak? Study body language and you can walk into a room and see what everyone's thinking and feeling."

"I suppose healers must know their patients well."

"Aye." He sighed. "I had another amputee today. Four this week. I hate that job so much. When I bring that cleaver down, I feel like an executor with a guillotine. I know these people will struggle, may well die very soon. I try my best to put them back together, but in reality, there's nothing I can do to help them. I may even prolong their suffering, a torturer with a medicine bag. If it wasn't for today and what we're trying to achieve, I don't know how much longer I could go on."

She put her arm around him, pulled him gently into a hug.

"I'm also concerned that there will be much more of that to come today. I've seen what happens when people revolt, Till. The people who get caught up in the fighting are ill-equipped, poorly armed, emotionally charged, and disorganised. Against well-drilled soldiers, they're like blind lambs in an abattoir. I know you've done your best to source weapons and armour, and we can only hope the General pulls through, too, but remember—thousands of people who join us won't be protected."

"I know. We'll look after them as best we can, after everyone. Remember what we always say, the words that began this whole thing."

Together we rise. "I know you will, Till." He smiled.

Dhijs's gaze turned to the harbour. The sun was beginning to burn through the morning mist. How soon would it be till the sky was filled with smoke?

"It has been no easy task, encouraging those who have felt so much pain to love and care again," Dhijs said.

"We lit the fires of hope within them, showed them another, brighter path. But for now, it is out of our hands. All we can do is trust that everyone does their jobs." Till's jaw was tight as she spoke.

"You're certain you still want to do this?" Dhijs asked, wondering if her nerves had weakened her resolve.

"With all my heart. There is one image in my mind that keeps playing over and over, and each time, it lifts my soul and refuels my desire."

"And what image is that?"

"The moment we stand upon the walls of the Keep in victory."

"And what of Vaso?"

"I look forward to the moment I sink my blade into him too."

11

They fell quiet, the cries of the gulls filling the silence between them

"All I'll say, Till, is not to let revenge against Vaso distract you."

She paused. "I know."

The conversation lulled. "I'll miss these mornings philosophising with you," he said at last. "For I imagine, whatever happens today, we won't be in a position to do this again."

It was her turn to smile. "You worry too much, Dhijs. Instead, you could think of us spending our mornings free, higher up the hill, looking out over the city that we helped to save. But yes, I will miss our mornings here too."

A bunch of starlings swooped down before them, and Dhijs threw them a few chunks of bread. They squabbled over it, pecking and screeching at one another. "I must take a tincture to a sick girl," he said. "The poor lass can scarcely catch a breath. Living next to those damnable factories spewing their smog has turned her lungs to glass."

"It's a sad story that's become too familiar," she said, shaking her head.

"The medicine does little to help them. They have spoken of leaving the city, moving away from the smog. But they have no coin to pay for such a thing. They are trapped, like so many others."

"Not to mention, why the fuck should they have to. Our government should be caring for them, making sure they're safe. That's their very purpose. But the deaths of the poor mean nothing. We're collateral damage, pawns in their depraved game of profiteering."

"Not for much longer."

Her eyes lit up. "Now we wait."

"And agonisingly so. Our friend in the union—are you sure you can trust him?" he asked.

"He's wanted this for a long time, as have his people. Maybe even more than us. They've been on the frontline of this struggle. Their spirits are crushed, but the fire still burns. All it takes is some fuel to stoke it."

"I trust you."

"And I you." She stood, reached into her cloak, and pushed something into his grasp. A dagger. "The day has come at last, my friend. Liberation. Stay safe and see you in a few hours." She kissed him on the forehead, and then she was off into the mist—perhaps the most unassuming revolutionary he'd ever seen, but the one they all needed.

The Worker

The cough rattled around Zia's head as much as it rattled around his son's lungs. The crackling wheeze. Over and over. Poor lad could scarcely breathe. His eyes were forever bunched in pain as he anticipated the next agonising spasm. There was little left of him now but skin and bone. Zia would do anything to stop the life being choked out of him like this. But there was nothing to be done. No relief but poppy milk for the pain. Too much of that would kill him, though. Sometimes, in the darkest hours when sleep wouldn't come, Zia wondered whether that would be kinder, wondered whether he was playing torturer, hoping for a miracle cure. Was it selfish? Wrong? They were questions he didn't have the mettle to ask another living person. Aloud, he'd put it to the stray cats in the alley and didn't like the sound of the words.

Arica dabbed Marty's forehead with a damp cloth. It was filthy, just like everything in this shithole of an apartment. A fresh layer of soot accumulated on the windows and sills each day. There was no point painting the walls; they returned to their black and grey state within a few days. Dust and grime clung to everything in Smog Town—that's what they called this part of Pietalos now. When Zia was young, before the factories, it was called Smotera, home to the fisher folk of the city. His pa and grandpa had been fishermen, and his ma had been one of the finest hawkers in the fish market, but Zia could never take to the trade. The constant rocking of the boat made him vomit.

Marty broke into a fit of coughing again. Arica placed a hand on his chest, as if trying to purge the pain from him. She clung to hope that Marty would recover, though her eyes told Zia it was waning. Marty grew greyer each day, his breathing like the grating of broken glass. It felt wrong to leave them both for work, but he had no choice. They were already behind this month and if they missed the rent again, Ilkar wouldn't just slash him up a bit like last time. He liked to leave his debtors "smiling," as he put it—a couple of cuts to either side of the mouth.

"I'll be back as soon as I can, love." He gave Arica a smile, and she returned it, but there was no warmth there, just tiredness and echoes of times fading from memory. He glanced into the broken looking glass by the door for his usual final check before leaving. His green eyes were puffy, dark rings heavy below them. He was the only one in his family to have green eyes. Growing up, his ma said it meant he was special, but nothing special had ever happened to him. He was small but wider than most men, unsculpted but harder than the anvil he bashed metal against all day. He didn't feel tough or hard today, though, and he needed to be, more than ever. He put his cap on his bald head and, head down, turned and left.

Rain pissed down on him the moment he stepped outside. He turned away from the miserable greyness and lit a cigarette. The first one of the day always brought a small feeling of relief. It was the only time he ever felt any semblance of it anymore. He set off, moving around the puddles that invaded the muddy road.

A drove of hooded workers, shoulders hunched against the rain, filed along the road, all heading in the direction of the looming monstrosities that were the granaries, ironworks, tanneries, slaughterhouses, mills, and everything in between. There was little chatter, little acknowledgement of each other. Horses pulled carts laden with barrels, rickety wheels splashing water over already sodden bodies.

At the end of the road, the silent crowd began to split. The children headed for the cotton and wool mills, their bodies small enough to move through and beneath the weaving looms. Scores of women, their heads wrapped in an array of colourful shawls, headed for the fisheries, where they'd spend the day cutting and gutting. Zia tacked onto the end of the crowd of bulky-shouldered men heading for the ironworks and tanneries. Someone barged into him, nearly knocking him over. A spark of rage flashed within him, before he realised who it was.

"You're a dickhead, Jhon."

"Good morning to you too."

"Wet enough for you?"

"Water and me get along well, Zia. My roof's been leaking for months. We've learned to coexist."

"That prick Samson still not fixed that? Fucking landlords."

"Don't even get me started."

"You should have mentioned it. How about I come round and we try and sort it?"

"Sounds good. How's Marty doing?"

Zia shook his head.

"I'm sorry, mate." He slapped his back and pried no more.

They moved into single file as they approached the factory gate, giving their names when asked by the sneering company official. He was flanked by a pair of brutish guards with truncheons on their hips, and were ushered through like prisoners being booked in.

"Oi, Zia." The thick accent and drawl belonged to a wiry man named Bert, who caught up to him and Jhon. "That prick Yoni isn't signing people in for their full hours."

"A few people have mentioned that," Zia said.

"Enough people for you to do something about it?"

Zia sighed. "You know what it's like at the minute, Bert."

Bert looked incensed. "I'll tell you what I *do* know—there was a time when you would have offered the bosses a straightener for pulling shit like this. I ain't sayin' it, but some people might get to wonderin' what they've got on you. Something big to dull the Hammer."

"Every time the union asks for something, they take something away and pile on more work. And you know what's on the chopping block next. Do you want that? Gods forbid, Bert, that an iron beam drops on your head and kills you. Do you want to see Aleesa and the kids penniless and left to be swallowed up by the city?"

Bert's fluffy brows furrowed and his jaw hardened. "I know. It's just that I don't know how much more I've got in me to keep going like this. And the same goes for the rest of the boys. You're a chief, and you gotta hear us. We can't take no more shit. People start askin' what a union is even for."

"I hear it loud and clear. And don't doubt the union. That's what they want everyone to do, and that's what will divide us. Imagine what it'd be like if there was no union. You'd be working eighteen-hour days with no break for pennies an hour like they do down in Usha."

The bell clanged. Bert huffed and shook his head and wandered off to his workshop, spitting as he went. Zia sighed. He gave Jhon a nod, a half-smile. Jhon didn't return it right away. They parted, Jhon to the heat of the forge and Zia to the shop floor. It pained him to see disdain in the eyes of people whom he considered friends. As Bert said, the men talked openly now about removing him and the other stewards. Gods knew what else they said about him. None of it was true, of course—Zia would rather return a coin purse to its owner than lift its contents. But they were frustrated, and the company structured things so all frustration was directed toward the union and its stewards, painting them as too weak to fight back. It ignored the reality: hours lost in those long meetings, arguing and arguing, threatening walkouts and strikes, being backed into a corner and forced to accept shit he then had to polish as gold to sell to the others. It was a battle to maintain what little rights the workers still had.

He used to have more energy, more get up and go to get behind the cause. Where'd it gone? Had age blunted it? It wasn't just work he was beginning to feel helpless in, but at home, too, with Marty and Arica. All he wanted was to make them smile, feel happy and safe. An impossible task. The fabric of his life was falling apart at the seams, and only a few threads kept it together.

The morning wore on and he bashed out his frustrations against the anvil. His mind wandered to the rhythmic beat of metal, to thoughts of Marty and Arica. He hoped they were okay. They'd be safe at home today, he'd decided. There was nothing to pillage in that part of the city. Besides, their most precious possession was slipping from their grasp. All he and Arica had ever wanted was a child, and now she had to watch their only one suffer each and every day, unable to do anything to help him. A dozen healers had visited Marty. They suggested different tinctures and methods, from steaming his face to meditation. Zia worked sixteen-hour days to pay for it all. And yet there was no improvement, only decline, and it correlated with Zia's deteriorating mental state.

He'd always been a patient man. Some in the union called him the Diplomat. It was how he ended up a gaffer. But of late, violence consumed his thoughts. He wanted to inflict the pain and suffering that he and his family and friends felt each day upon those causing it—the cold-hearted company he worked for, his jobsworth of a boss, Freeth, the corrupt government that allowed it all to happen. It was all borne out of helplessness, he knew, a way of feeling powerful when he felt so weak. For a while, apathy had doused the flames before they could do more than flare. But then he met Shadow. Everything she had said, everything she had promised was everything he wanted—hope for a better future, control over their own lives, fairness, justice, and protections for workers, who would even get a stake in companies. When she shared this with him his heart had fluttered like it had the first time he'd kissed Arica. How could he refuse? But the bigger question was, could he do it? Over the past weeks, doubt had infected his thinking. Rousing himself from bed each day was like climbing a mountain. How could he inspire his coworkers if he couldn't inspire himself? And he'd yet to figure out a way of rallying everyone behind him.

"Zia!"

The shout cut through the clangs and bangs. He looked around and saw a young lad called Birken beckoning him. "Hurry!" He was a jovial

18

sort, and his jug handle ears complemented that well, but there was no humour in his expression now. Just eyes wide with worry.

Outside of the workshop, Birken revealed more.

"It's Cheese. He's... not good." Tears glistened in the young lad's eyes. Zia saw streaks on his cheeks where the wetness had cut through the soot. Cheese was older than Zia by a decade, and for as long as he knew him, he'd had the name Cheese—acquired for his body odour. Ulfa was his real name. He worked in the forge, charged with supervising the team that hoisted the huge cauldrons of molten steel. That could mean burns, a crush, maybe a heart attack.

Zia stepped into the suffocating heat. Cheese's relentless screams filled the room. It didn't take Zia long to see what had happened. An iron chain thicker than a strongman's arm hung limply from the ceiling, its final link bent and broken. Below it sat the great iron cauldron that should have been held aloft. Around the iron bowl was another group. Some stood away, hands on their heads. One young lad had passed out and was being roused by another. On the ground, a few patches of vomit were drying in the heat.

They'd stopped the furnaces, but Zia's tunic already clung to his skin. The prospect of seeing what injuries had befallen Cheese didn't help, either. The group parted, and there, on the floor, he saw Cheese. Or the top half of him, at least. From the groin down, his legs lay under the cauldron. An inordinate amount of blood had fled his body and left him looking pallid and drained.

"Has someone sent for the doc?" Zia said.

"Aye, Little Byll went sprintin' off for him," said a pug-nosed man named Palea.

"We need to get this fucker off him," another man said. He was called Fish, small and stout with a thick moustache.

"We do that, he could bleed out," Zia said. "Anyone got any moonshine?"

A few small skins were thrust in his direction. "Someone roll him a cig," Zia said as he knelt down beside Cheese. "You're gonna be alright, lad," he said, stroking his sweat-laden forehead. Out of the corner of his eye, the growing pool of crimson inched closer.

"Fuck me, Zia, it hurts. It fuckin' hurts."

Zia gently lifted his head up. "This will help. Fish brewed it, though, so it tastes like piss." Through gritted teeth, the poor bastard drank.

"It does n' all," he managed to say, and those around him laughed, nervousness mixed with relief and hope.

"The doc is on his way, lad. Got a cig here for you."

"I'd rather a line of spice," he croaked before coughing up blood and grimacing.

"Wouldn't we all." Zia looked around him, but everyone shrugged. He wasn't surprised. Spice fiends weren't known for being sharers, only shafters.

"Deep drags on that now, lad. It's all gonna be okay."

Cheese blew smoke and cried out as pain wracked his body again. Zia held his hand, gripped it tight. Told him over and over it was going to be fine. Knowing in his heart it wasn't.

"Zia, tell Jinny I'm sorry."

"You've got nothing to be sorry about. And you can tell her yourself when we get you out of here." Zia smiled and patted him on the shoulder, but Cheese's eyes were no longer focusing on Zia.

"We'll have to think of a new nickname for you now, Cheese," Zia said, holding the cig to his lips once more. Cheese closed his eyes as he inhaled and never opened them again. His trembling body stilled. His fingers went limp. Zia bowed his head and held onto his hand, hoping he'd come back. The cig burned down to his fingers. He dropped the butt, looked at Cheese's face, whiter and purer than anything in this shit-stained city, and wiped the tears from his eyes.

"How did it happen?" Zia said, trying to push the emotion out of his voice.

"Cheese was guiding us when that chain snapped. He jumped in and pulled little Rocky away, but it landed on his legs," said a young man named Ant.

"I told 'em! I can't believe how many times I told 'em. That chain was *fucked*. It needed *sortin'*, and look what's happened," shouted Fish.

Others jumped in then, but a few started pointing fingers at each other for not following it up, for not making sure the chain was fixed. Zia pushed into the middle. His deep voice cut through the rabble.

"There's no point fighting among ourselves. That's what they want us to do. We all know who's responsible."

"And who is responsible, Zia?" a piercing, high-pitched voice said from behind them. Zia turned to find one of his least favourite people—Freeth, his supervisor and a jobsworth in a class of his own. The rat of a man had never lifted a hammer, just scurried between the workshops and reported everything he saw back to the management. Beside him was the doc, a man he knew—Dhijs. He gave Zia the slightest of nods before hurrying over to Cheese. Freeth came to stand before the group of workers.

"If you don't speak, you'll get a lashing," he said with a sneer.

"It's nobody's fault but yours," Fish said, his eyes red with tears. "Cheese was a good man. He didn't deserve this. Three weeks ago, I told you about that cracked link, and every time I brought it up, you said we couldn't afford to stop to fix it. That we were working too slow and losing the company money." He jabbed his finger in Freeth's direction as he spoke, his voice raising with every word.

Freeth's eyes flashed with rage. "So you're saying I dropped that cauldron on him?"

"You might as well have done, you little prick." Fish stepped up to Freeth, towering over him.

Freeth licked his lips. "All you union men are the same, thinking you're a gift from the fucking gods. You're all just pieces of shit like everyone else. It's a lashing for all of you for letting this happen." He drew his whip faster than a knight drawing a blade and cracked it against the

21

ground. "And you'll remember to be grateful you've got this job, unless any of you want to fuck off out that door? I've got hundreds of fellas just like you waiting to take your place. How about it, Zia? Fancy quitting today? Or are you still trying to keep that half-dead kid alive?"

"Fuck you," Zia spat.

The whip snapped forth and struck him across the chest. It tore his shirt and cut open his flesh, the wound burning like acid. Before he could raise his hand to it, another blow struck, and then another a couple of heartbeats later, striking his shoulder and back. Zia sank to the ground, bunching into a ball for protection.

"Hey!" "Oi!" came his colleagues' shouts.

"You want some, too, you little shits?" His eyes held a wild look. "Get the fuck back to work or you'll get worse than the sack!"

Hands helped Zia to his feet. His fellow workers patted his back, reassured him, surrounded him. And then, together, they moved toward Freeth. Fear broke through that wildness controlling him. Zia could see it in his beady eyes. Those at the front of the group charged. Zia found himself barraged forwards, towards Freeth's prone body, as dozens of feet stomped, kicked, and crushed his pale, ratty face into a pulp. Zia felt nothing at all at seeing his tormentor killed, just stinging pain from the licks of his whip.

Whistles sounded; the guards were coming. There was a time when this place had no guards, no whips, no beatings; a time when they were trusted to work. But he supposed he saw this coming, with everything the company owners had done. Cutting pay, cutting numbers, longer hours, making them work shifts through the night, on the weekends, forever threatening them with the sack. And of late, refusing to fix things when they broke, which risked all of their safety. Poor Cheese had paid the price. How many more would have to suffer because of their neglect and disdain for the working man?

Freeth was the punch bag with which his colleagues vented their frustration. But they weren't done.

"It's time we teach these fuckers a lesson," a big, broad-shouldered man roared in his booming voice. A chorus of angry shouts met it. They charged forth, shoulder to shoulder, as if on the battlefield. The guards turned and ran, one or two with piss trailing down their breeches. Seeing their fright made Zia feel alive, powerful—feelings he often fantasised about having. In control of his life rather than being thrown about left and right. And in that moment, he realised he'd achieved what he needed to today. He'd incited a riot, or rather, Cheese's death had. And now he just had to make it spread.

"To the boss's office!" someone shouted.

Zia spoke up. "No. We need to get everyone else first. We stand together. They can't beat us then."

The group of twenty or so metal bashers shouted their agreement in unison. And then they were off at a run to the next shop, and the next, beckoning their colleagues to down tools and follow, though many took their hammers with them. Any jobsworth who tried to stop them took a beating. Zia watched on, not stopping them, not condoning them. It's not how he would do things, but his colleagues, his comrades, had suffered over the years. This was their turn.

The factory employed about five hundred people, and now the vast majority gathered in the main yard.

"We want change!" was the mantra that bounced off the brick walls of the different workshops. Zia found himself at the front with two other gaffers from the union. To his left was Bykol, a tall, wiry man well into his fifties who didn't say much, but what he did say always left an impression. And at his other side was Arta, Bykol's junior by twenty years, with an infectious smile and charm to match. They exchanged a nod. Zia had spoken of a moment like this with the two of them before. None of them had thought it possible—they'd thought everyone's apathy ran too deep. But people could only take so much before they snapped. Together, they led the group to the boss's office.

They gathered around the original smithy that had since become the head office, chanting and stomping their feet in time. The door remained shut. No movement at the windows. Zia and the other two union leaders stepped up and knocked. The crowd fell quiet. No answer. They knocked again, louder.

"Just kick it in," someone shouted. It was met by a chorus of "yeahs." Zia looked back at the crowd and then proceeded to plant a heavy leather boot against the wooden door. It swung open on its hinges, and they stepped forth into the musty room, only to find it empty.

Papers lay ruffled on a desk to their right. Empty chairs stood at angles around it. In the far corner to the left was a safe the size of a child, the door ajar. When Zia heaved open the heavy iron and looked inside, it was completely bare, save for a single silver coin.

He stepped outside, holding the coin, and looked at the expectant crowd, who watched him intently.

"This was all they left in the safe. All they think we're worth as human beings. These cowards have run away and taken their gold, gold that's covered in blood, the blood of our own!" He shouted the final words with the anger that coursed through his veins. The crowd fell quiet as death.

"One of our own died today. And it could have been avoided. These greedy bastards chose to let it happen, and they'll go on doing so till all of you are cold in the ground. This is cowardice of the highest level. It's a symptom not just of what has happened to our industry but of a campaign of oppression waged by the elite against us working people. They want to crush our spirits, break our resolve." Zia punched his palm. "They want us to be grateful for shit work while forcing us to work harder for less. They take away our rights, our protections from fuckers like our bosses. They sit in their manors and halls while our people die from the smogs that choke the streets, that suffocate our children. The smogs that they cause! All they care about is the gold in their pockets. Well, I say enough is enough. It's time to take that gold off them. To tear apart the hideous machine that they've created. It's time for us to take back what's ours, what our own hands have built. Otherwise, we don't have a future, and neither do your kids. What we know and love will all be gone, just as it's fleeing from us now. All we'll be left with is regret, regret that we didn't do something when we could. So I say this—pick up your hammers. It's time to take to the streets and take back this city."

The roar was deafening, yet over it, his orders carried. "Hit the other factories and spread the word. Chant the words that make the rich-born shit their pants—the working man rises!"

They began to chant those final words, a battle cry that imbued them with strength and belief. And with it, they went, fanning the flames of discontent.

The Pusher

Shouts roused King from a deep sleep. Not the normal calls of the dockers and workers passing by outside, but angry shouts and statements packed with aggression and malicious intent. He opened his eyes, rubbed his temples to appease the emerging headache, and loudly expelled from his arse the gas that had built up overnight. A grumble sounded next to him. He lifted the blanket, took a look at the scraggy frame, the thin black hair, the badly healed scars on her back. Be damned if he could remember her name. He remembered little nowadays, apart from what mattered—who owed him money.

King swung his legs out of the bed, scratching the itches provoked by the straw mattress, and opened the shutter of the room's only window. The view wasn't much—straight into an apartment in the building opposite, no more than spitting distance away. As always, Nosy Niho hung out of his window.

"What's happening, Niho?"

Niho shook his head. "Been shouts and bangs like this for the past half hour or so. Think it's coming from the factories."

"The factories, you say? You thinking a protest? Them union fellas love a moan."

The stooped, grey-haired Niho shrugged his shoulders while he watched King roll a cig. King sparked a match on the window ledge, took a pull, and threw the lit cig across the alley before starting on another. Niho caught it with more deftness than his decrepit frame suggested him capable of. Not long after King had moved in, he'd learned that Niho would sing like a bird if you gave him something—a cig or ale, usually.

Niho took a drag on the cig as if his life depended on it. He nodded his thanks to King. "Could be. Not been one since they banned protesting, though."

"How many died in that last one? Couple hundred?"

"Three hundred and twelve."

King spat down into the alley. "Murdering fucks."

"That's one way to describe them."

King studied his neighbour as he leaned out the tiny window, craning his neck to see what was happening on the road beyond the rubbish-filled alley. Niho was a fiend for gossip. But other than that, King didn't know much about the man.

"What was it you said you did, Niho? You know, before you ended up here?"

"I was an architect."

"Like designing buildings? Damn. What happened?"

He twitched, neck spasming, left eye flickering. "I saw something I shouldn't have. And rather than risk me saying anything, they disgraced me. Framed me for the crime they committed. And I can prove it. I've got the evidence, if you wonna see it?"

"What did they say you did?"

"Raped a woman I worked with."

"That's what you saw someone else do?"

He nodded and took another long drag on his cig. "My boss, it was. She was just a kid. Her first week in the job."

"Sick fuck," King said. "Give people an inch in this town and they take your soul."

A huge bang blew away their conversation. Niho nearly dropped his cig. The windows rattled. A few panicked screams echoed toward them from the main street.

"Let me go and see what I can find out, hey, Niho."

"Be careful, King."

That drew a smile from King.

"Oi," King said, pulling the blanket off the bed. "Time to move."

The naked woman groaned. He still couldn't think of her name.

"What's all the racket outside?" she asked.

"Kick offs down at the factories, maybe."

She turned over to reveal a pretty face. Her eyes were dark and intense, thin lips curling into a mocking smile. "Reckon there'll be looting?"

"And what will you be looting?"

She shrugged as she stood and slipped on her homespun dress. "Whatever I can make some coin on."

King laughed at her ruthlessness. But his mirth didn't linger. Trouble was bad for business. A big disruption had the potential to put a hefty dent in cash flow. He took a deep drag on his cig and handed it to her to finish.

King washed his mouth out with a swig of last night's mead, threw on his dark woollen jerkin and breeches, pulled on his boots, and donned his long purple cloak. Even though its colour had dimmed with the grime of the city, he liked how it contrasted with his usual dark attire. Plus, everyone had come to recognise him for it. With recognition came respect. He grabbed his dagger, gilded hilt glistening in a way that pleased him. He'd won it playing cards with some rich-born, and it too drew respect, especially if held against someone's neck.

King locked the door to his shitty apartment with his lady friend in tow. There was nothing of value inside, but people still tried to break in, even though they knew King lived there. That's how desperate they were. Or stupid.

They stepped onto the street. People ran past them, heading for the factories, where a roiling cloud of black smoke rose over the tenements.

"I hate to ask, but what did you say your name was again?" he said as he lit another cig.

"Fuck you, King," she said, shoving past him.

28

King laughed, blowing smoke into the cold air, and set off in the direction the crowd was headed. There'd been heavy rain, judging by the puddles invading the road; now it was drizzling. Despite the weather, the streets were packed, and it jarred his senses. This time of day, people around here were either at work or still abed, fucked after the ale and root of the night before. He moved onto the main street leading to the factory district, and froze. A river of bodies marched toward him, a deluge of working men and women chanting and singing, beating iron plates, pots, and pans.

"Enough is enough!" The cry, repetitive, bored into his head. "E-nuff is e-nuff."

King had never seen this many people protesting all at once. It was as if every factory in the city had emptied judging from the overalls and grimy faces of the smithys, the sawdust-stained breeches of the carpenters, the white hats of the bakers and millers.

"Long live the unions," King muttered to himself. He took another deep drag on his cig right as a sharp blast of a horn sounded to his left. Sprinting toward him were a mob of guards, armed with rectangular shields and spear poles without their spearheads—still a weapon capable enough of caving in a skull, but not as lethal as their pointy variations. They were designed to club an enemy into submission rather than kill them.

The guards looked fierce in their conical helms, covering their whole faces save a slit for their eyes, and their big and broad pauldrons and chest plates made them seem more imposing than they were. King stepped back against a door, not wanting to get caught up in the carnage that was about to unfold. The guards passed him by, though a few gave him hard looks from beneath those anonymising helms. King reciprocated.

The guards made a dense line across the road, shields locked to form a wall.

"Forward!" The order, and their boots, began to pound the ground in time. The marching workers didn't waver. A small man with the thickest arms King had ever seen started shouting words of encouragement.

"Don't let them scare ya. I can smell their piss and shit from here."

The thousands behind him roared and then they charged. King grimaced as the two lines struck with a bone-crunching clap, the sound reverberating off the apartment blocks that loomed on either side of the street. Cries of pain rang out. The dense wooden poles rose up and down, bashing and striking, the harsh hands of power hammering down upon the people.

More than a few protestors grabbed onto those poles and used them against the guards. And they had weapons of their own too—hammers big and small, iron bars, and heavy iron balls, projectiles manufactured for war, hurled by the craftsmen who wrought them to cave in helmets, break bones, and bludgeon bodies. One or two guards were pulled out of the line by the rims of their shields, and the protestors poured forth into the gaps. This wasn't just a march to get back some working rights or a few coppers more an hour. This was a battle. And they were prepared to kill for the cause.

The guards began to break. The status quo was well and truly fucked. A thousand thoughts assaulted King's mind, things he'd have to sort, arrangements to make. It was time to go.

King hotfooted it down the side street, past his apartment block and onto a quieter street that ran parallel. He needed to get to the Warren and warn the others. And as he went, he tried to rationalise things.

A more organised and bigger group of guards could quash the protestors, especially with blades and crossbows, and life would go back to normal. But in his thirty-three winters alive in this godsforsaken shithole of a city, he'd never seen people fighting for their lives like that, and when they lost that fear, well, the respect his purple cloak garnered would mean nothing. Subdued was how King knew them. Too tired from working, too broke to enjoy life, or too drunk or high to give a shit about anything. It

30

was perfect for the government, King was sure. Maybe even deliberate. Why else let the pushers run free, minus the token arrest when someone wound up dead? Why else let people work to death for coppers in the factories and fields? When they got hurt doing crazy, unsafe jobs, they either wound up destitute or paying a visit to people like King. Smoke a bit of root and their woes eroded, at least till it wore off. And then it was back to reality, to the open prison that was Pietalos, to a life devoid of hope, of prospects of anything better.

People didn't get hooked to root; they yearned for the escapism it offered. And the government criminalised them and their unhappiness. Root was just the symptom, and a profitable one at that.

King looked over his shoulder and ducked down an alley beside a disused warehouse. Halfway along, he came to a rusty old drain cover. He stomped on it twice. A dozen heartbeats later, it lifted an inch.

"It's King. Hurry up, Mal; there's something going on."

The iron ring opened wider to reveal a young girl, no older than ten summers.

"What is it?" Mal asked, her ice-blue eyes regarding him amid a face forever smeared with soot and grime.

"Out the way. You'll hear in a second. Who's in?"

"Just Vic and Sika."

King almost stepped on her fingers as he started down the ladder. But Little Mal was fast, the quickest of all the kids he had in his employ. Her eyes and ears missed little, and her slight frame meant she could sneak into crevices no one else could, which made her all the more useful. She was annoying, though. Too smart for her age, and that made her a cheeky little brat. She'd taken a fair few beatings because of it—not from King; he wouldn't beat a kid. Kicks and punches had no bearing on her mouth, though. All that changed was the look in her eye, like a killer plotting revenge. She may have been a kid, but he didn't doubt she'd figure out a way to do it.

The usual stench of damp and age-old shit hit his nostrils. The abandoned sewer had never been cleaned, just left once it was decided it had no use anymore, like everything and everyone else in the city. King had never understood why they'd stopped using it—the structure was solid and well-built, which couldn't be said for most of the houses aboveground. But he couldn't complain; it made for a fine hideout, and its location was ideal—just on the edge of the main area of root-riddled tenements, and secure and hidden enough to keep out any unwanted visitors, like rioters or guards.

They moved along a narrow corridor before stepping into a large room with a vaulted ceiling that was once used for storing maintenance equipment. Lit and warmed by braziers around the edges of the room, with further light provided by stolen chandeliers and their many candles, it now served as the gang's main hub. Vicor was sat at the long table, eating, as usual; stew, judging from the gravy dripping from his bushy grey beard.

"You keep stuffing your face and you'll never be able to run from the guards."

Vicor swallowed a mouthful. "They have to catch me first."

King smiled. "You seen what's going on out there?"

"No. Not long awake, to be fair. What's the scoop?"

"You wouldn't believe it, Vic. The workers are striking. Well, more than just that. The guards came to calm them, and they fought back. They killed a bunch of them."

He sat up in his chair. "Shit. What kicked this off?"

"Be damned if I know." King sat down and poured himself a mead from the pitcher beside Vicor.

"Something must have happened."

"Maybe they're all just fed up," said Mal. The pair of them turned in their chairs to Little Mal, standing at the edge of the room drying some clay pots they'd used for breakfast with a rag.

"Of what?" Vicor asked.

"Of life here. Don't you think it's shit?" Mal said as if pointing out the obvious.

"It's not so bad," Vicor said.

"For you, maybe," King replied.

"What do you mean by that?" Vicor said, frowning.

"Just look at your situation, Vic. You're an established pusher. You've got pockets so full of jingling coins they pull down your breeches. And no one messes with you 'cos you're a crazy fucker." Vicor nodded his approval of the last comment. "The point I'm making is there ain't many people like you, Vic. Most folks have got to work in those gods damn factories, or out in those fields, or on that graveyard of a river. Those who don't try a straight life end up whoring themselves or hooked on root or whatever shit that will help them forget just how miserable life is."

"Dammit, King, you're a ray of sunshine today," Vicor said.

"It's just how it is," Little Mal said.

"No one's talking to you," Vicor shouted, throwing his bowl at her. It missed, smashing against the wall.

King glared at him. "Pack it in, dickhead." If he was closer, he'd have clipped the fat wastrel round the ear. "She's right, or are you pissed off that a kid is smarter than you?"

Vicor shook his head, boxing his anger into a mutter. King glanced at Mal. She had her head down, cleaning up the broken pottery. He'd have to watch Vicor later. The fat oaf would blame Mal for King chastising him, and King had seen him do bad things for a lot less.

"Anyway, how was last night?" King asked.

"Average. People are piss poor. Usual faces still, just less often. Trying to make it last, see."

King narrowed his eyes. The earnings had dropped off the past few weeks, if not months. A general decline. It made him uneasy. Growing up, he'd been cold, hungry, homeless. His ma had been a baker. His pa had worked on the docks but died in an accident when he was a boy. His ma died a couple of years later. Baker's Lung, they called it; death by slow suffocation. And when she couldn't work anymore, they couldn't pay the rent. That's how it started for King, working for the older pushers, making coin to pay the bills. And he fell in love. Not so much with the job but with money and the security it brought. His ma died in the end, but he was able to pay a doctor to make her comfortable and give her a good funeral. And then he was on his own. He left that life behind, even his birth name— Curtys. His gang became his family. Except Vicor. Vicor made his skin crawl.

"When the rooties don't have coin to buy my shit, my pockets are empty and my enterprise ain't growing an inch. That means I ain't happy and I gotta start asking questions," King said.

"What can we do about that, King?" Vicor asked.

"It's a good question." He lit a cig. "The rich-born overcomplicate things, but it's simple. If you ain't got no money, you ain't spending shit. And that means no one's making coin, not even the pricks up the hill with their taxes. The business I do should be easy. Buy for a coin, sell for two. Everyone gets something. It's a fair swap. The problems start popping up when you get these bankers thinking they're clever by lending fake money to their rich friends. Then they use the money to buy up all the property in the city. Next thing you know, prices start going up and more people end up on the street 'cos it costs more than a person can earn in a year to pay for some box room in a rat-infested tenement. No wonder they're all kicking off out there."

The sound of footsteps on the stone floor caused them all to turn.

"Who's kicking off?" Sika took a seat at the table. Her sharpness was plain to see; a quick look at those alert brown eyes told you everything. King could trust her more than any of the other louts he employed. That's why she handled the count.

"The workers are *revolting*," Vicor said with sarcasm.

"They're always moaning about something," she said, running her hand through her short, bleach-blonde hair.

"Nah, this is different. I'm pretty sure they killed some guards," King said.

"Good news for us," Vicor said, dismissing the news.

"You sure about that?" King asked him, a little sterner than he'd have liked, but the fat bastard was grating on him. "Yeah, there might be a few less fuckers to harass us, but there'll be a dozen more to fill their boots before you know it. Nothing about what I saw is good for business."

"I think you're over-egging things," Sika said. Vicor laughed.

"And let's say it doesn't stop there. What if this government gets overthrown? I'm sure we'd all be out in the streets partying like everyone else. But long-term, what does that mean for us, this enterprise?"

Vicor grumbled. "You've got your head in the clouds, King. It's just a bunch of tanners moaning about wages. How are you jumping to revolution?"

"It depends on who rules in their place," Sika said, ignoring Vicor. "Another group of the same corrupt bastards could come in and everything will go back to normal. Humans are creatures of habit. I think we know that better than anyone. But King is right. Maybe they won't like us pushers—not that anyone does now. But maybe the streets get cleared up and we end up dead or in jail. Or on the flipside, they legalise it all and we become legitimate business people overnight. Anything could happen."

King could see some kind of moral revolution taking place as well as a political one. Not that he could comment much about morals. He knew the effect root could have on a person. But the people he sold it to were fucked before they came to him. They were looking for a way out, an escape. And that's what it gave them—a slow, euphoric ride into the bright white aether. Some people might even call him a shaman, a healer of sorts. 'Caring for the wounds of the soul.' Some whore had said that to him once. Others would—and often did—call him the devil. The pusher of poison. Who'd have thought the root of such a common mushroom could have such devastating, wonderful, and profitable effects?

"You're right, Sika," King said at last. "Who knows how this will play out."

A deep rumble rocked the walls, the floor, the ceiling. Dust and stone fell upon them. The cups and jug rattled on the table.

"The fuck was that?" Vicor said.

They were all on their feet now. King's eyes were fixed on the ceiling, gauging whether it was going to hold. "Sounds like the strike has escalated."

"Want me to go look?" Mal asked, nonchalantly moving toward the doorway.

"No. I need you to do something for me." He turned to the other two. "Here's the plan. We take what we can, stash the rest, and lock up this place. We're too close to the heart of this shitstorm, and I don't doubt the mob might go looking for pushers too. We'll head to the safe house on the edge of Tewbrucke, by the city wall. That should be far enough away from the action. We'll wait it out there."

Sika and Vicor nodded. No hint of objection in either of their eyes.

"Mal, you get that?"

She nodded. She was a clever kid; of course she got it. "I need you to find Bein and Uter. Tell them to round everyone up and head to the safe house. It's on Griffin Row, opposite the bakery. Head down the side alley and you'll see a stairway that leads to the basement. Go there and give the usual knock. Got it?"

She nodded, and without a word, she was off. Fuck knows what kind of carnage he was sending her into, but he'd sooner let her go than risk his own neck. He wasn't afraid to admit that. Like he wasn't afraid to admit that he wouldn't lose sleep if he never saw her again. She was just a useful piece in the game of trying to make enough coin to survive.

The Urchin

Mal ran as fast as her legs would take her. She wasn't sure what caused the explosion, but as she hurtled down the alley, a sweet burning smell filled her nose, like the oil they used in fancy lamps. Over the tops of dilapidated buildings, she could see thick black smoke swirling, blocking out the cloudy sky. Lots of people were moving about on the street ahead. Some of them carried torches, poles, planks of wood. She slowed to a stop and hid behind a wooden bin, watching, observing. That was what she was good at—studying how people behaved. It helped her work out whether they were a threat or not. The way these men shouted, the way they thrust their weapons into the air, it was all too aggressive. And it scared her. But she had to get past them. Not because King had ordered her to. But because she had the information she needed for Shadow.

Fear didn't drive her on; it was love. Unlike King, Shadow had been nothing but nice to Mal over the year she'd known her. She'd fed her, cared for her when she was sick. In exchange, Mal gave Shadow information on King and his crew and the things she saw on the street, something she was all too happy to do. They were a bunch of heartless cretins, and she was old enough to know that the stuff they sold wrecked people's minds and lives. Working for them wasn't a choice—she'd tried to flee, and they'd tracked her down and beat her for it.

She told herself it wasn't all that bad. Alone, like how she was after Bryn died, she was weak and vulnerable. With them, they sort of had her back—when Vicor wasn't stomping on it. Oh, how she despised that fat bastard. Once, Vicor beat her so much it took a week for one of her eyes to open again. Her vision was still a little blurred. After that, she'd tried poisoning his food but hadn't added enough. He spent the best part of a day in the privy shitting out his guts. A small consolation, at least. But soon Shadow would deal with them, deal with them all. First, Mal had to make sure the gang was where they needed to be.

The flow of bodies began to trickle. Mal made her move, darting across the road and down the dark alley opposite. She hurried on, quiet as a mouse by instinct after years of avoiding bigger kids and spying for King. Before the opening to the next street, she hunkered down behind a pile of rubbish and junk. She peered through the gaps in the debris. It appeared clear, so she risked a bolder look. Nothing right nor left except for a trail of broken wood, the glass of broken windows, rubbish blowing about, and the odd small fire from a discarded torch. The protestors must have moved through here not long ago. Shouts and cries echoed off the buildings, and away from them she moved, ducking down another alley and heading for the west side of Tewbrucke. It was a good distance from the factory district and further down the hill which the city sat upon, so she hoped the escalating protests hadn't touched there yet.

Her hopes were dashed.

The closeness of the buildings had masked the cacophony beyond, and she stepped out into the heart of a battle. A line of guards tried to beat back a surge of people. Most were men, but there were women, too, and boys and girls not much older than herself. As King had described it, they all fought with a rage-filled intensity she hadn't witnessed except in the pushers who beat her. One woman's head exploded as a spear butt pummelled into it. A guard lost his footing and was promptly stomped to death. Iron poles, hammers, axes, and anything else that would serve as a weapon beat against the guards' shields and bludgeoned limbs and bodies when they found a target. Rocks, stones, and glass bottles sailed through the air. All around her, crimson stained and spattered the faces, hands, and clothes of scores of people. Blood poured from wounds, eyes hung out of sockets. Demented wails of agony, anger, and anguish filled the air. She could feel it all, and it put an extra step in her stride.

Mal sprinted across the street, behind the battered line of guards. She jumped over rocks and glass bottles that crashed down in front of her. Chancing a glance back at the fighting rabble, a rock struck the side of her head. She fell to the ground, head spinning, ears ringing, the coppery taste of blood in her mouth. A warm trickle ran down the side of her face. Touching it, she saw the red of blood and felt like she might vomit. But she didn't. Further dabbing revealed that the cut wasn't big, and it only throbbed a little. Her head cleared, and the need to escape struck her as hard as the rock had. She got to her feet, unsteady at first, but made it to the nearest alley.

At the end of the alleyway she checked her wound again. The bleeding seemed to have stopped, though her hair was now a matted, sticky mess. The throbbing had eased too. She peered out into the street like a rabbit poking its head out of its burrow. It looked clear, but further down the road, she saw smoke and flames coming out of the first-floor window of an apartment block. It was a stash house. Not one of theirs but known to everyone about. Like King had said, the pushers were a target now too. Mal had already known as much, though she didn't tell him. Shadow had asked her to find out where the gang intended to lay low. As Shadow put it, "To kill a monster, you have to chop off its head and destroy the roots of its corruption so it never comes back."

Mal went in the other direction of the burning stash house, then ducked down another alley. She didn't feel anything at the thought of King and the others being killed. They beat and hurt her, abused her, used her. They often made her steal from hard-working people, which she hated. And one time they made her stab a man in the leg with a little knife. They said it wouldn't kill him, but it still hurt him, more than she'd ever hurt anyone. In between these activities, she spent her time thinking of ways to get revenge.

Shadow promised Mal justice, as well as a heart that cared for her, food, shelter, hope of a better life. She was just like her ma. Mal had even called her that once by accident, but Shadow just laughed. She was kind like that, forgiving. It was a far cry from the life Mal knew, the life where if she dropped a jug of mead, she'd end up black and blue.

Mal moved along the alleyway without a sound. It allowed her to listen out for any danger up ahead. And she heard something that caused her to stop—murmured voices. Sniffles. Mal crept closer, heard a female voice, and judged it was coming from a window in the wall on the right. One of its panes was smashed. With one eye she peered inside. In a rocking chair in the corner of a well-kept room, a mother held in her arms a sobbing girl, no more than two or three summers old. She sung softly to her, swaying her child from left to right. The mother looked up, right at Mal, who scurried away like a thief caught in the act.

Sometimes when sleep wouldn't come or when the hunger pangs kept her awake, Mal thought of her family. Ma had died not long after Pa had run off with the coin they'd made catching pigeons to get her the medicine she needed. That meant they didn't have any coin to bury her, so some men put her on a cart and wheeled her off. Mal wasn't sure where they took her. She was just glad her tears had obscured the sight of it trundling away.

They couldn't find Pa, so it was just her and her older brother Bryn after that. The landlord soon kicked them out when they stopped paying rent, and Bryn couldn't hack it on the street. He got sick real quick, and to make some coin, Mal began working for King. It was just easy things at first, like standing somewhere and keeping an eye out. Then it turned into causing distractions, like starting fights or pretending to be injured. But all of that paid for Bryn's medicine. He got better, then worse, until one day she woke to find him cold and still. She'd never felt more lost than she had at that point. After losing Ma and Pa, she still had Bryn. Once he was gone, she had nobody. For long days, she'd done nothing but cry, and the hunger only made things worse. But in the end, that forced her to get up and forage and hunt. Focusing on surviving helped distract from the pain, the loss, the loneliness.

The nooks and crannies of the alleyways came to an end, as did her thoughts of the past. A wide space lined with broken cobbles stretched out before her. An eerie quiet hung in the air, thick as the sweet-smelling smoke that shrouded all but a few feet in front of her. The din of the riots played a constant tune in the background, broken by the barks of dogs or a random, unnerving scream. She turned down a side road and picked up the pace, her destination close.

The smoke wasn't as thick here, and as she moved along the street, it thinned to swirling wisps. The house marking their corner came into view, a two-storey building with cracks running down its walls and thick weeds growing out of the roof. A magpie, perched on one of the branches, flew off when she neared. She gave it a salute, as she always did when she saw a lone magpie. Her ma had said it was bad luck not to, and she couldn't afford misfortune now. As she neared the building, she saw that the upper windows were broken, and those on the ground floor were boarded and marked with purple graffiti—the calling card of King's gang.

A shape laid at the foot of the steps to the house. Her eyes stung from the smoke, and her vision was still blurry from Vicor's last beating, but soon recognition struck. It was Becker, a towering, broad-shouldered man who walked around like he owned the place. The size of him, few people could argue otherwise. He wasn't moving, his face turned away from her. Her steps slowed to a creep.

"Beck," she said.

No reply. A fly rose up from his body. She spotted blood on the steps, dripping down the stones. Mal touched his shoulder. His head dropped toward her, and she jumped back and turned away. His face was a bloody pulp, nose caved in, eyes a gelatinous mess. At the top of the steps was a wooden walkway that led to the front door. Two pairs of legs stuck out from behind some dumped wooden furniture. More blood pooled on the ground. That was three of them dead then, but there were four here in all.

Dodging the blood, Mal opened the door into the stash house. Light broke through the boarded windows and revealed a dingy room with grotty walls, broken chairs, and a crooked table. Slumped down in one of those chairs, blood staining his jerkin from a stab wound to the gut, was Ulenda. His eyes fluttered open at the creak of the floorboards. He grunted.

"It's Mal," she said. He coughed, choking on his blood.

She approached but kept a safe distance. "What happened?" she asked.

"Bastards jumped us," he managed to say. "Get me a healer." He hawked and spat blood.

"Who got you?" she asked, wondering if it was Shadow.

"Fuckin' randomers. Rooties. Peasants. They rushed us, took everything. Get me a damn healer," he shouted.

This man had done nothing nice for her. Why did he deserve her help? "Go to hell," she said.

"You cheeky little bitch," he growled and lunged for her. Mal hopped back and watched as he fell to the ground in a writhing mess. She left him coughing up blood and bile.

Outside, grey clouds had returned to smother the sky. The stench of fire hung heavy on a breeze that chilled her cheeks. A few raindrops touched her arms. She set off at a run once more. She could think of nothing but one thing—she was free. At last, no more King and the gang. For the first time in a long time—not since she, Bryn, Ma, and Pa had been together—she smiled.

"Oi."

Mal fell to the ground. A man had jumped out before her and pushed her down. Pain throbbed in her back and arse, but the wild, unfocused look in the man's eyes took her attention away from that.

"You with this lot?" another male voice asked. He stepped into view from behind his companion, bone-thin with a toothless smile, gazing down at her like she was a juicy steak.

"No," Mal said.

"Liar!" he shrieked. "I've seen you before. He grabbed her shirt, pulled her close, the stink of rot on his breath threatening to knock her out. "Take us to the root or we'll gut you like we gutted your mates."

He dropped her and pulled out a rusty, blood-stained shiv. King was right to fear the people rising up against the pushers. Maybe Shadow didn't need to do anything at all.

"C'mon, kid, take us," the other rooty said, hard to understand with his tongue rot and lack of teeth, her least favourite side effects of root. "We'll give you your fair hit."

"Shurrup, will ya!" the other said.

Their gazes on each other, Mal seized her chance. She scampered past their legs and set off as fast she could.

Mal didn't stop to check if they were following. Just kept running. She rounded a bend and was met by the cries of women and children echoing off the apartment blocks. Further on, she found crowds of people gathered outside a burning building, trying their best to douse the flames. None of them were taking part in the riots, it seemed. They were its victims, if anything, those hiding out, hoping for it all to end, for the trouble to pass them by.

The attempt to douse the fire was a poor one—only a few leaky buckets, and the nearest fountain was down the street. The fire spread, licking over adjoining buildings. More panicked people streamed out of smoke-filled doorways, carrying what little belongings they had. Babies and toddlers cried. Adults held their heads in their hands, bodies shaking with sobs. What would they do now? They were homeless, possessionless. Who would help them? Not their neighbours. The people around these parts of the city were cold. Mal couldn't blame them, though. Everyone was fighting to survive, to put food on the table and keep the roof above their heads. Shadow would help them, though. She thought of these kinds of things and no doubt had a plan.

Mal scurried around the edge of the crowds, but it was a challenge to get through the dense, stinking press of bodies. An elbow struck the side of her head. A woman with a massive rear end bounced her into another woman, who shoved Mal away to bounce into someone else. Another limb hit her head where the rock had struck. It knocked her dizzy, vomit churning in her gut. The noise, the smell, the heat; she couldn't breathe. Bile rose up and gushed out of her mouth. It was met with shouts of outrage and disgust. People around her moved away. Relief at last. She staggered on, her vision settling, so too her stomach. She slumped down against a wall, breathing ragged. Her ears rang like bells, her skin was clammy, but her panic receded. The urge once more began to take control—get to Shadow. *Then you'll be safe.*

More fires burned in other buildings, thick grey and black smoke pluming out of windows. And more people were out on the streets, more innocents not wanting to get caught up in what was unfolding, but through no choice of their own, they were. From the youngest children to the oldest adults, the events of the day wouldn't leave anyone untouched. Mal had heard Shadow say as much. She had said for it to work, everyone must rise up, not just a few. And everyone *must,* for their own sake. Their will had been broken, their spirits crushed. *This will restore it,* she had said. Mal believed her. She trusted her. There was no one else like Shadow. Shadow remembered the people society had forgotten, like her crippled sidekick Gerida and the street urchins like Mal. She genuinely cared, which in a city as cold-hearted as Pietalos was rarer than finding gold in the rivers of shit that flowed through its streets.

Mal took her time, picking the safest route. She managed to break free of the crowds at last and joined the road that led to Shadow's hideout. Up ahead, a huddle of people stood before the doorway of a tenement, her vision too unfocused to see who. Her heart dropped when she neared. It was Tam and his cretinous followers. The little prick worked for Vicor, and he'd beaten her more times than Vicor ever had. Her heart pounded against her ribcage. There was no other way around; she had to get past them.

A flame caught her eye. One of the gang smashed an apartment window. The fireball followed, and the group of boys and girls cheered as if they'd just found a fat purse of coin. Like a cat, she began to move, hugging the buildings opposite, her eyes never leaving the cheering group who whooped as the fire grew. Level with them, the fire took hold and rushed out of the window.

"Let's do more," said Tam in his stupid, monotone voice. Mal froze, hoping they wouldn't see her.

"Look who it is, fellas. Mousy Mal."

"More like a rat."

They laughed.

"Get her," Tam said.

Mal moved before they did—a vital head start, for they gained fast, their legs longer than hers. But sanctuary was in sight. At the top of the alley leading to the meeting point, she saw a couple of Shadow's people. She didn't know their names, but Mal never forgot a face. The tall one was thin, a hungry-looking kid—she knew the type well. But in the heavy cloak and leather jerkin and breeches Shadow had given him, he looked tough and intense with his hawk-like eyes. The other kid was a few years older, just as thin but taller and broader. They saw her coming, drew their bats, and gave her the slightest of nods—keep moving.

A looming brick wall flanked her left, an apartment block to her right. The alley was like any other, full of sacks of rubbish, broken glass and pottery, and bits of wood and old furniture. Halfway down, a head appeared out of a door in the building to the left. It disappeared quickly, but Mal knew who it was. She ducked inside and found Tieren standing there, sword hanging from his hip. She'd never seen the old man armed before, which told her whatever Shadow had planned was big. Expressionless, he turned and scampered off down the corridor. Mal knew to follow.

They stepped out into a wide, open factory floor, or what once was. It was devoid of work benches now, just a collection of dust, refuse, and cobwebs. A few broken windows near the top of the room allowed in slithers of light, enough for her to see the open drain cover up ahead.

45

"You know the drill, kid," Tieren said, stopping and stepping aside for her.

Mal looked up into his small, blue eyes, and nodded. "Good luck today," she said.

For the first time ever, she saw the corners of his lips curl into a smile. The master thief had somehow survived for sixty years on the street. Some said he was raised by the rats and cockroaches of the city's sewers, for there was no putting him down.

She clambered down the ladder. This old sewer was part of the same abandoned system that King and his crew hid out in, but much of it was blocked and isolated by crumbling tunnels. The passageway to Shadow's main hideout was usually quiet, save for the odd rat. Today, it was packed with people, all standing shoulder to shoulder in the light of staggered torches upon the walls. Mal looked up at them in bemusement; they returned the stare with hard expressions. They wore metal armour on their chests, legs, and arms. Some carried helmets, others shields. She saw swords and daggers, spears and axes. There were archers, too, wearing leather rather than metal. Their bows were twice Mal's height, and she looked up at them in wonder. A woman holding one caught her eye. She smiled. Unused to the kind expression, Mal gave an awkward smile back and hurried on to the central room where already she could hear the din of voices coming through the illuminated doorway.

Mal slowed as she stepped inside. The adults stood around a table in deep conversation, their backs to her. She could just see their hair—brown, blonde, grey, some a bit of both, short and long, neat and unkempt. And at the head of them all was Shadow. Though she was a foot smaller than those around her, she carried a presence that others deferred to. Her emerald-green eyes forever moved, stopping only to linger over the person speaking before scanning the room. She locked eyes with Mal, gave her a smile, and nodded in the direction of the far corner of the room. A group of other kids sat on the floor eating fresh fruit. Mal's belly contracted at the sight. She hadn't eaten since yesterday morning.

Mal targeted the basket brimming with apples, pears, and plums. She kept her head down, careful not to draw attention, and grabbed one of each, as well as an extra plum for later, and retreated to a spot away from the other kids on the cold stone floor. A few of them spoke to each other, but most looked like loners. Mal knew Shadow worked with other kids to get information, but she never knew there were this many—a dozen and a half, at least. All different ages, a mix of boys and girls. They were all thin, just like Mal. Twine and string kept up poor-fitting breeches, with ragged shirts and hole-ridden jackets on their backs. Most had no shoes, and those who did had more holes in them than a moth-riddled blouse. A few had injuries like Mal, cuts and scratches on their grimy faces. One girl had a bandage wrapped around her arm, a blood stain seeping through.

As she looked around, Mal began to recognise faces from different gangs, kids who had developed reputations over the years; on the street, such a thing could be a shield to protect you or a target on your back. That was true for Peg the Punch, who Mal was surprised to see. She was a few years older than Mal and was known for running crews of kids for some of the bigger gangs. Peg got her name after punching another kid in the arm and breaking it. Mal suspected the arm broke more because the kid was weak and underfed. Either way, she didn't want a dig in the arm from Peg, so she averted her gaze and chewed her apple. She shuddered at the bitterness, but it was juicy and not too soft. Nothing worse than a soft apple; she'd eaten more than a few, and not through choice.

Raised voices and hurried movement over by the table signalled the end of the adults' meeting. Some of them left, one or two giving orders to others who then ran off to spread the word. Mal always wondered what it'd be like to have that kind of power, to tell someone what to do and off they went and did it. Her whole life, she'd been bossed around and made to do things for others. Her pa always sent her out on errands and beat her if she was ever late returning. And then she was left to be bossed around by King. But not anymore. Now she was here with Shadow; safe, she hoped.

47

Shadow approached her and the other children with a few men Mal recognised. She bore a warm smile upon her face, her arms outstretched as if attempting to embrace them all.

"Thank you all so much. Did everything go to plan?" she asked them.

Heads nodded; a few kids murmured confirmation.

"Excellent," she said, clapping her hands, her grin broadening. It was infectious, and Mal felt her own lips curling into a smile.

"So all that's left to do is to tell these good men the information you have and then you can keep on filling your bellies. You can of course go your own way too, but there's trouble brewing in the city, as you well know, so if you want to hide out down here with all the food, you can. It'll be safe and warm here."

Mal looked at the other kids' faces. Some nodded, pleased at the prospect. Some looked like they needed more convincing, brows furrowed with distrust.

One of the kids, a timid-looking boy a few springs older than Mal, spoke up from the back of the group.

"Are you going to hurt them, Shadow?"

"Of course she is," Peg the Punch answered for her. "And she's going to do it because they're bad people. They hurt us and everyone else." Shadow didn't answer, her face expressionless.

"Shadow, what's going to happen to us after all of this is over?" another boy asked, his voice breaking as he spoke. His cheeks flushed when some of the other kids looked at him.

Shadow's gaze wandered over them all, taking in each of their faces as a mother would her children, and then she spoke.

"When this is all over, there's no going back to the streets. There's no returning to your life working for pushers and having to steal to eat. You'll have homes; you'll have food and people to look after you. Today is the final day of the struggle that your short lives have been so far. And tomorrow is the start of your lives as they ought to be lived."

Nobody, it seemed, knew how to respond to that. Shadow gave her companions a nod, and they stepped forward and started speaking to individual kids. They had paper and quills and scribbled down the details the children had to share on their respective gangs. The kids who had injuries were tended to as they recalled their intel. An older man with wrinkles on his forehead and bushy white hair knelt before Mal. He had a sponge and a bowl of water in his hands.

"My name is Dhijs," he said.

"I know you. I bought medicine from you when my ma was sick."

He smiled and dabbed at the cut on the side of her head. The cool water tickled her ear. With a gentle touch, he washed her hair, applied some aloe gel, and bandaged her head. "Doesn't look too bad at all. I'll come check on you in a little bit," he said before moving onto another hurt kid. Mal liked him, she decided.

"How are you feeling?" Mal hadn't heard her approach, but she knew her voice well.

"I'm okay. Better now I'm here."

"Tell me, Mal. What did you see?" Shadow asked.

Mal looked up into Shadow's eyes and felt at ease.

"It was a bit... scary. The rooties killed some of King's gang, and they tried to get me too. And there's lots of fighting everywhere. The guards were trying to hold all the people back, and they were beating them with sticks and poles, but then they were getting pulled down by the people and beaten to death. There are lots of fires as well. I saw whole buildings burning and people outside crying. All their stuff is gone. Are you going to help them?"

"Of course. Anyone who has suffered will be helped and healed. We do not forget anyone. Everyone moves forward together. That is the way it needs to be, and after today, it is the way it *will* be." Shadow crouched down so she was eye level with Mal. Shadow caressed her cheek and stroked it with her thumb. "Thank you for your help today, Mal. You don't need to worry anymore." Shadow pulled her into a hug. No one had hugged her since her brother Bryn. Tears came to her eyes, but she sniffed them away. She couldn't let the other kids see her crying.

"Any other questions?" Shadow said with that warm smile of hers.

"Who are all those men in the tunnels?"

"Shadow!" someone called from the doorway. She half-turned, acknowledging the young man, who looked to have an urgent message for her judging from his shuffling feet. Shadow turned back to Mal.

"I have to go. Stay here, stay safe, and tomorrow, I'll be back, okay?"

"Don't get hurt," Mal said.

Shadow laughed.

The Protector

An eel of tension writhed in Kishto's gut. He'd used the privy before they left the station, but nature called again. He cursed his sensitive stomach. No turning back now, though. No choice but onwards.

Kishto brought up the rear of the group. Four of his comrades moved ahead of him, split in two rows. Everyone held their shields high, spears half raised, waiting to strike. The further on they went into the heart of the trouble, the thicker the smoke became, reducing visibility to all but a few feet. Kishto's eyes stung and watered, visor and helmet doing nothing to keep the smoke or the smell of charcoal at bay.

His comrade Bugs, named for his favourite pastime of crushing insects, started coughing. Not a slight clear of the throat but deep, barrel-chested huffs.

"Pack it in, Bugs! Every fucker in the city will know we're here," said his other comrade, Bakor, sergeant and leader of the group, not through competence but a panache for corruption and willingness to do bloody work. He was a sadistic prick with a fat, bald head that made him look like a testicle. Kishto hated him.

"He can't help it if he coughs, Bakor," sniped the man to Kishto's right, Gevere. He'd joined their group only a few months ago and hated Bakor from the off. Gevere was tall and thin but stronger than he looked. He was about a decade younger than Kishto and seldom spoke, which made Kishto wary of him. Quiet men unsettled him. It often meant they were hiding something, that to speak might run the risk of exposing it. Despite that, Kishto enjoyed the cutting comments he hurled at Bakor.

Their fat commander scowled, put down his visor, and turned back around. The final man making up their company was Lightning Myke, ironically named for his slowness in both mind and body. He followed Bakor like an abused mutt and kept quiet whenever his leader spoke.

Bugs's coughing under control, they continued on, following a narrow street with tall buildings on either side—shops and stores on the ground level with apartments above them. A magpie cackled somewhere, the mocking sound echoing off the walls. Bakor jumped at the sudden noise.

"Damn fuckin' birds," he muttered, hawking and spitting on the ground.

Kishto scanned the tiny windows of the apartments, seeking threats. It wasn't uncommon for projectiles to rain down on patrolling guards. Sometimes heavy, sometimes sharp, oftentimes stinking. But the shutters he could see through the smog were almost all closed. People must be hiding, trying to ride out the chaos, the chaos they had been tasked to control. The reports that had filtered back to the station were bleak. As the afternoon wore on, it became clear that this was no ordinary protest. The hearts and minds of the people held ominous intent. Dozens of guards had been killed, hundreds maimed. Scores of protestors had died too, yet those deaths hadn't dissuaded their march. Each one added a bomb of fuel to the fire. And it riled up his colleagues as well, some of whom had lost their friends. Now they were on the streets with angry and murderous thoughts in their heads, men conditioned to abuse their power, to think that they were a cut above the people they had sworn to protect and serve. What had been a protest had quickly turned into a battle, a fight to the death between the state and its people.

As his fellow guards reacted to the developments, Kishto became curious about his lack of sorrow at hearing of the deaths of his colleagues, at the brutal details of what was done to their bodies. If anything, he found himself smiling, glad of the news. He hated these people. He hated this job. He hated the man it had turned him into.

When he had joined the guards as a spotty teenager, his driving force was to help and protect other people, especially after what had happened to his sister, Mara. That's what the guards were for—he thought. He soon realised that wasn't the case. That "to protect and serve" was a strapline, a front. The guards were a gang, organised and legitimate in the eyes of the law, and worst of all, funded by the state. None of his colleagues was honest, and as Kishto began to witness their dishonesties, they began to level threats at him to keep his mouth shut. Kishto still remembered the first dressing down he received from a superior, the spit flying into his eyes, the point of the knife against his throat, blood trickling down his skin. "Tell anyone of this and I'll cut open your ball sack, rip out those fucking raisins, and shove them down your cock-sucking throat." That man was Captain Vaso, an odious snake who'd slithered his way up the ladder. The corruption that emanated from him oozed throughout the organisation.

They turned onto a narrow street, the buildings looming over them like old oak trees. "It's quiet," Bugs said. Always one to declare the obvious. "Remember that place, Kish?" he asked, nodding at a boarded-up shop front.

Kishto hadn't until Bugs pointed it out. A side hustle that'd gone wrong—taxation of a local baker. He got cross about having to pay taxes to the local gang, Kishto and Bugs, *and* the state, said he had no coin left. Kishto hadn't believed him, so he'd roughed him up a bit, broke a few fingers. Still no coin, so he beat up his wife and son. Nothing. That pushed the baker too far. He'd grabbed Bugs's dagger and came at Kishto like a mad dog. Kishto had no choice but to put him down. The wife and kid too. No witnesses, Bugs had said. Kishto had done well to block that out of his mind until now. A few nights of solid drinking in the days after it happened had helped. Shut down the thoughts before they could take root. Banish the images, discard them like paper. That was how he got by each day, how he slept each night.

"Bugs, you natter like a damn fishwife," Bakor spat. He halted their progress, looked all around him, sniffing like a hound. "Gaffer said they needed us at Hylda's Square. Where's that from here? Can't see a pissing thing with all this smoke."

Kishto thought they were heading east, but he couldn't be sure. He looked up, trying to glimpse the sun, but beyond the smog, the grey sky offered little but the threat of rain. Kishto hoped it held off. He hated the patter it made against his helmet. The sound bore into his skull like a maggot tearing into rotten flesh.

"I think it's left here," Lightning Myke said. No one paid him any attention.

"Let's just keep heading straight on. When we find the next high street, we'll go uphill. That's where the fuckers will be heading," Bakor declared and marched off, his pace renewed. Myke scampered after him. Bugs and Gevere turned to Kishto. They both looked at him with uncertainty. They were wandering like blind men through a battlefield. No direction, no clue where the enemy was. And having Bakor as a guide made the matter worse.

"Stay close," Kishto said, and they continued on. They came to a wider street that led up the hill to the richer parts of the city. The smoke was thicker now, black, grey and white from the fires burning around them in shops and apartments. Kishto could hear children crying, women calling out names, screaming in pain, in despair. It always troubled him, that sound. Reminded him all too much of the night his sister was murdered. The look on her face one of pain, of terror, of knowing her fate. And the wails that came from her mouth as that fucker pulled her red hair and stabbed her over and over again in the gut. He'd gotten her pregnant, a married man, a young star rising up in the world of Pietalos politics. Kishto had come downstairs at the height of his fury. He was ashamed to say that he had hidden, waited for the blood-soaked attacker to leave before he brought himself to observe the carnage. That was the one image he couldn't drink away.

Before they died, he had promised his parents he'd look after Mara, and look what had happened. Maybe it was through guilt he joined the guards, to prove that he *could* protect people. Though after twenty years in the job, there was one thing he'd learned about himself—he was shite at protecting anyone but himself and the interests of the state and the wealthy.

Bakor slammed his spear against his shield, bringing Kishto back to the present. He stopped and turned to face them. "I can hear 'em up ahead. Weapons at the ready." He pulled down his visor and continued on at a jog, their armour rattling as they went. Through the swirling white smoke, they saw flashes of movement—people ducking into doorways, the shutters of windows closing.

"Be ready, boys. This could get ugly fast," Bakor said.

A slamming door dragged Kishto's gaze from the rear to the right flank. As he turned, he saw scores of feet scurrying away from them beneath the smoke. They looked like women and children, but he couldn't be sure who was friend or who was foe. Kishto and the others held back while Bakor marched on. He disappeared into the smoke. Kishto's focus returned to the rear when a scream erupted—the high-pitched wail of a girl. It died in her throat.

Kishto's heart battered his ribcage, trying to flee in its fear. Sweat formed at his brow. No matter how often he heard screams like that, they always had the same panic-inducing effect. He took deep breaths, steadying himself on his spear, and pushed visions of Mara's dead body out of his mind. Bugs, Myke, and Gevere set off at a run, and Kishto followed. They found Bakor with his back to them, spearhead painted red. Kishto looked past him to see a young mother and her daughter on the ground. Crimson stained the woman's clothes around her gut. The child's clothes were stained red too—right in the back, struck as she was fleeing.

"What the fuck did you do?" Gevere spat.

"They attacked me!" Bakor shouted, rounding on him.

"What, a woman and kid?! What could they have done to a fat fuck like you?"

"Watch your mouth, cock nose, or I'll bounce you back to wherever the fuck you came from." Bakor pointed his spearhead at Gevere. For long moments, the pair exchanged furious stares, chests heaving with rage. Bakor broke his gaze first, seeking allies in Kishto and Bugs. Disdain coursed through Kishto's veins, and he didn't try to hide it as he locked eyes with Bakor.

"Don't look at me like that, Kishto. I've seen you do way worse than this." Bakor gave him a wicked grin.

Kishto fought to contain himself. He'd become good at hiding it, at suppressing it. But seeing that poor woman's blood-stained clothes, hearing the screams, brought back memories that sent anger coursing through his veins. Bakor became that murdering politician. Kishto strangled the shaft of his spear as one thought alone consumed his mind. Judging from the intensity in Gevere's eyes, he was thinking the same. Kishto willed Gevere to sink his spear into Bakor. But Gevere broke his gaze with the fat little man. He looked at Kishto, a lingering look that Kishto held, and though nothing was said, they understood.

"You hear that?" Bugs asked.

"The drum?" Myke said. It was growing louder.

"Aye. The fuck is that?" Bakor said.

"Sounds like the one they have at the slinging matches," Lightning Myke said in his droll voice. He seemed unfazed by the situation. But he was right. It did sound like that—the same beat the hardcore fans used when their team was playing, something they brought home from the war with the southerners decades ago. The *dum, dum-dum* played over and over, filling Kishto's ears.

"Get to that apartment block," Bakor ordered. The one thing Kishto could credit Bakor with was his rat-like survival instinct.

Backs to the wall with the door to an apartment behind them in case shit got out of hand, they held up their shields, forming a wall. Bakor,

Bugs, and Myke stood at the front, with Gevere and Kishto flanking them. Through the narrow gap in his helmet, Kishto tried to take in as much as he could. But all he could see were shadows growing around them in the smoke. He caught glimpses of masked faces, of poles and sticks, hammers and scythes. Nobody spoke. They were here to do a job and keen to get on with it. And judging by the coughs, the sniffs, the shuffling of feet, and the tap of weapons against palms, there were hundreds of them. Kishto's heart began to pound in a whole new way. He began to think he might die. From the smells and sounds emanating from his comrades, he guessed they were thinking the same.

"What are we gonna do, boss?" Lightning Myke asked Bakor quietly.

For once, Bakor had no response.

"That door open?" Bakor asked.

Gevere tried the handle. "No."

Bakor cursed. "Kill any fucker that comes close. We put a few down, and the rest will shit themselves."

Gevere glanced at Kishto, but something flew out of the smoke that left them all ducking low.

"Something hit my shield," Bugs called out as the sound of cracking wood rang out.

Heartbeats later, a swarm of projectiles flew at them—rocks, wooden blocks, bottles. Kishto buried his head beneath his rectangular shield, shockwaves from the relentless blows running up his left arm. He decided against stealing a glance. Myke couldn't resist a look, however. He poked his head up and took a brace of rocks to the face. One made light work of his noseguard. The other put a dent in the side of his helm. In stunned silence, he fell onto his back, eyes vacant, legs twitching, blood running down the side of his face.

"The fuckers killed Myke!" Bakor roared. He moved toward the rioters. Bugs tried to grab his arm, missed. Seeing the two of them start forward, the rioters reacted in kind. Dozens began to charge, and chaos erupted.

Despite being a fat little bastard, Bakor's spear arm was strong. The broad and wicked blade shot forward, cutting through flesh, muscle, and bone. He left half a dozen on the floor, most of them crying out in pain, a couple lying still. Bugs was at his side, lashing out with his spear too. Gevere, like Kishto, held his ground and kept his spearhead clean.

The rioters backed off after seeing their comrades downed so easily.

"You're murdering scum," one man shouted, his face covered with a blue scarf. Dust covered his brown jacket, and in his hand, he held a heavy iron bar, which he pointed in their direction.

"Just like you, then," Bakor snapped back.

That sparked a chorus of angry shouts. People spat as they roared, feet leaving the ground with the force of their barks. Kishto had never seen such hate in the city's people.

"How can you fight for these bastards up the hill? You're meant to protect us!" one man called.

"Fucking pigs!" yelled another.

"Murdering rats!"

The crowd's anger again spilled over into action. They charged, and Bakor and Bugs lashed out. Kishto pulled his blows, careful not to land them, seeking to drive off his attackers. To his right, people screamed and piled up on the ground. Bakor shouted like a man victorious after a battle with honourable foes, not one with armourless peasants.

The rioters backed off again, and the same man as before spoke up, only now his face was visible and spattered with blood.

"You don't have to serve these fuckers. You're victims in this as much as we are. We've all got a chance to unite against them and take back what's ours. To give ourselves a future instead of an early fucking grave." Those around him shouted in agreement. "Throw down your spears and join us. Help us take down these bastards and take back our city!"

The cheering grew louder still. Kishto looked at Bakor, then Bugs. Such a decision was more than their simple, conditioned minds could process.

"You're not like those two," Gevere said, leaning in close. "I'm with them." He nodded at the crowd. "Are you with us?"

Kishto frowned but it soon softened when he looked at Bakor, hurling insults at the crowd, gesturing at their dead and fallen. He hated him so much. Hated everything he stood for. He embodied the guards—the opposite of protectors. Here they were, roaming the streets, slaying innocent people. The rioter was right—who were they helping but the people who created this mess of a society? Who gave the guards a mandate to act like the criminals they were said to be stopping, who turned a blind eye to the murders, the beatings, the rapes, the disappearances, the extortion? This was not what he wanted when he became a guard. He'd suppressed the moral conflicts within himself for so long. He could blame it on fear, but that would make him selfish, foolish, a coward, too afraid to stand up to bullies. Just like when Mara was killed. He might not have been able to save her, but he should have done something to stop that rich bastard, to get some justice. But now he could. Now he had the ability to actually help the people he was sworn to protect.

Kishto gave Gevere a nod. He turned his focus to Bakor. With a firm boot to the back, Kishto pushed him forward, off balance, into the crowd. Bakor landed on his front, dropped his spear and shield, and within a heartbeat, he was lost to a sea of kicks, stomps, punches, and gouges. Gevere took a more direct approach with Bugs, plunging a dagger deep into the side of his neck. He wiped his blade on Bugs's jerkin. Kishto had liked Bugs more than the others, but seeing him murdered didn't move him an inch.

"What now?" Kishto asked him.

Gevere had a broad grin upon his face. "Now we overthrow this godsforsaken government!" He patted him on the chest and walked forward to greet the rioters, some of whom approached him, embracing, shaking hands, slapping backs. Questions were asked about Kishto as eyes turned upon him. Their mirth died as they waited for an answer.

"He's with us," Gevere said. "Aren't you, comrade?"

Kishto looked at him, then at the crowd, at the expectant and hostile look in their eyes, at the bloody, fleshy mess that was Bakor, then down at his yellow tabard, at the shield and axe emblem of the guards. He grabbed the badge and tore it off like he was ridding himself of something foul. The crowd erupted, and Gevere and his companions closed around him, cheering. Gevere sidled up to him, and threw an arm around his neck.

"If you really want to know what we do next, we need to get past the inner wall. You know the hidden door by the old servant's gate? That's where we're headed. All we need to do is knock, and when they see our uniforms, they'll open that door nice and wide. You in?"

Kishto took in the scene around him. He'd become a part of the uprising he'd been sent to quash. He'd helped kill his superior and conspired to kill another. It was a death sentence as far as the law of the land went. But he didn't feel as if he'd done anything wrong. For once in a very long time, he felt like he'd done some good. And now he had a chance to continue that, to build upon that warm feeling growing in his chest.

"Aye, I'm in. There's a shortcut we can take, just up here and to the left."

"Aha, that's the man."

"Gev, tell me this. Was this always the plan or did you just switch sides?"

"What do you think?"

"You were always too quiet to work out."

"And what does that tell you?"

"It was the plan all along."

He smiled. "I'm a revolutionary, brother. All of us fighting here are. Today's the day we take back our city, take back control of our lives." He grew more animated as he spoke, slapped Kishto's chest as he said the final words. "Stay close now; we need to show the others the way, and there are more of us to meet."

Gevere told him to give his spear to one of his comrades, declaring it was "all close quarters from hereon in." Kishto drew his shortsword and they set off at a run down the cobbled streets, a horde of men and women at their back—the two guards, protectors of the people, leading the people into battle.

More than once, Kishto caught sight of several of his colleagues' prone bodies, surrounded by pools of dark blood. Could he still call them colleagues? Had he ever considered them that? They were vultures who'd sink their claws into his back without a thought if it meant bettering their position. But that had been him too. He'd preyed on the weak just like they had. It felt fraudulent to switch sides after doing so much wrong and for so long, but it was also the surest he'd felt about any decision in his life. *Now is a chance to make amends*, a voice within him said, a voice that sounded like his Mara's.

At the end of the street, they came to a large building, a community hall where the local administrators held shop. Outside it stood another large group of rioters—mostly men with some women and a few fresh-faced youths among them. Soot and grime covered many faces. A few bore wounds or had blood spattered upon them. At the head of the group stood a small yet stout man wearing a flat cap. His two hands rested on the butt of a sledgehammer, the large iron block balancing on the cobbles before him. He held up a hand to Gevere in greeting.

"Zia, good to see you," Gevere said.

"And you, lad. You recruit another?"

"Aye, this is Kish. He's seen the light, and he'll help us get through the gate. The fellas on the door know Kish better than anyone."

Zia turned to Kishto, appraised him up and down. He looked as tough as an iron ingot, and his bright eyes held the sharpness of an arrowhead. "It's reassuring to see that one of you lot has a conscience."

Kishto couldn't help but bristle at the comment, even though he knew the truth of it. His sense of morality was as fucked as the crims they dealt with every day, if not more so. But this was a new day, as everyone kept saying. A time to start making different choices—positive choices.

"There's a bunch of lads up at the gate already. Pawdy said the bastards are sticking them good with arrows, so we need to get a move on," Zia said.

"Where is the one-eyed prick?"

"Gone to get a battering ram."

"Where did he get that from?"

"He said he built a load for Shadow. Had a gang of carpenters working on them after hours in the workshop. Knowing Pawdy, they'll do the job."

Kishto's ears pricked up at the mention of Shadow. The vigilante was the bane of every guard's existence. Rumour had it, Shadow was a woman. She and her gang targeted guard houses as often as they did the dens of root dealers. Flash attacks and raids were what they were known for—sneaking in, killing a few, and letting in the rest of the crew to finish off whoever was left and steal whatever held some value. Then they torched the place so it couldn't be used again. They could turn a place over in minutes.

Both gang lords and Kishto's own bosses raged about her, demanded her head, and promised huge bounties to whoever brought it to them. His main boss, the red-faced Captain Vaso, the nastiest prick of them all, had declared that he wanted to strip the faceless Shadow naked, march her through the streets for all to see, whipping her as she went, before hanging and drawing her body in Republic Square and sticking her head on a spike above Bastard's Bridge.

But hearing that a man called Pawdy had been making battering rams changed things. That meant she wasn't just some vigilante or gang leader. She was thick into this riot. Or, as Kishto was beginning to realise, this orchestrated revolution.

The inner wall loomed over the buildings surrounding it. Up ahead stood the gate, the threshold barred by an iron portcullis standing before dense wooden doors. Upon the dirty-grey parapets above, a host of guards leaned over the edge with bows and crossbows, loosing at will at the crowd gathered below. With so many closely packed bodies, every shot landed and sparked panic. People barged and shoved and trampled one another to get free.

"This is getting ugly," Gevere said. "We ain't far. Just up here and to the right."

They hurried down a side street and up a narrower one to the right, hundreds of eager feet clapping the ground. Kishto could see the wall at the end of the road. Gevere slowed them to a stop.

"Me and Kish will go alone from here. Listen for the signal," Gevere said to Zia.

The little man nodded. "Good luck, lads."

Gevere looked back at Kishto as they made their way along the road. "You good?"

Kishto didn't answer right away. In all honesty, he didn't know what was going on in his heart and mind right now. He felt dispossessed of himself yet sure of his actions. "Aye."

"Good man. Here's the plan. We run to the door and bang on it all panicked. When they see the two of us beaten up, they'll have to open up. We tell them we were jumped, and once we're inside, we kill them. Don't frown like that, Kish; there's no other way. We only get one chance at this. And come on, you can hardly say you like any of those raping, murdering bastards?"

When he chewed on Gevere's words, he couldn't spit out an objection. The long-haired man went on:

"Once we get that door open and our boys inside, we need to get upstairs and open that portcullis. Then it's a job of opening the doors and clearing the walls."

"Easy," Kishto said, humourless. He was trying to work out how many guards would be inside. The first door they could take with ease, he imagined. There wouldn't be more than two or three defending that—the door blended in with the stone wall, after all. The real throng of defenders would be on the walls, in the winch room and behind the gate itself.

"Ready?" Gevere asked. He didn't wait for an answer, slapping Kishto's chest and setting off at a panicked run—in character right away. He staggered his steps, hung his limbs at awkward angles, feigning injury, fatigue, shock. Kishto copied, his hobble less dramatic. Gevere made it to the door and began to bang upon the false stones.

"It's Gev and Kish. The bastards jumped us. Bakor, Myke, and Bugs are dead."

No response. Gevere looked at Kishto, concern and indecision in his eyes. He made to bang on the secret door again when it swung open.

"Crisp, thank fuck you're here," Gevere said to the man standing in the doorway.

"What happened to you two?" Crisp asked.

"They jumped us bad, Crisp. Bakor and Bugs are dead. Myke, too." Gevere hobbled inside, Kishto behind him. Crisp closed the door and barred it.

"You the only one here?" Gevere asked.

"Aye. They're all at the wall. The rats are trying to bust their way through." He laughed in his goofy way. "Too stupid to realise it's never gonna happen."

"I wouldn't be so sure about that."

The laughing stopped. "Why's that?"

"For the cause, brother."

In a flash of movement, Gevere leapt forward and plunged a dagger deep into Crisp's gut, twisting it and pulling it free. Crisp said nothing. Just gasped with shock and what looked like unbearable pain.

"Finish him properly," Kishto said, frowning. He hated letting a man linger on the precipice of death.

"Does he not deserve to suffer for what he's done to our people? What you did too?" Blood dripped from Gevere's dagger. Kishto couldn't help but notice it was pointed at him.

"Death is suffering enough."

Gevere's eyes narrowed, but he moved to Crisp and shoved his dagger under his chin, killing him instantly. After wiping his blade on Crisp's jerkin, he looked at Kishto with an uncomfortable sternness. "Remember this, Kish—there's no room for mercy in revolution. Did they show us mercy when they lorded over us? When they took away our jobs, kicked us out of our homes, stole the food from our mouths? Did they fuck! There can't be any half measures. Got it?"

Kishto bit back his next words and nodded. Gevere looked at him, sizing him up, before turning to the door, undoing the bolt, and kicking it wide open. With two fingers in his mouth, he gave a loud, sharp whistle. One echoed back in response, and a few heartbeats later, Zia and the others came streaming around the corner. They piled into the doorway—a hundred at least—and set off along the dark corridor, heading toward the gate. Gevere, leading the way, drew his shortsword. It was a matter of speed now. They had to overwhelm the defenders, raise the portcullis, and get that gate open.

They reached the winding stone stairway that led up to the winch room and further beyond to the parapets. From above, they could hear the excited shouts of the shooters on the walls, the cries and screams of those they wounded and killed. The plan from here was simple.

The group split in three. The largest force, led by Zia and his sledgehammer, headed for the gate. The others set off up the stairwell in single file, making as little noise as possible, before splitting in two. Half the group continued to the walls to clear the shooters. The other half went with Gevere and Kishto to take the winch room.

The corridor was lightless but Kishto knew the layout of the place well. At the end of the passage, he saw a light. The shadows of moving bodies flickered in its glow. The door to the winch room was heavy, with thick bolts on the inside. If those inside discovered them and decided to close it, they'd be screwed. Kishto picked up the pace, and those behind him followed suit. He kept his eyes on the threshold, switched his sword to his off hand, and drew his dagger, readying the smaller blade for a throw, just in case someone saw them.

Twenty paces away now. He could see the edge of the winch and chain. But he was conscious of the rattles and patters his new comrades made. As much as they tried, they couldn't move in silence—there were just too many of them.

"Hear that?" Kishto heard from the room ahead. Raised voices followed. They were onto them.

Kishto lifted his dagger, aiming for the doorway.

A young man with a pale face stepped into view. His eyes widened, his mouth opened, and a shout ripped from his lungs, only to die in his throat as Kishto's blade sunk deep into his chest. Kishto thanked the gods that he fell forward into the doorway, preventing those inside from closing it.

"Come on!" Gevere roared behind him. Kishto had his shortsword in hand again. He jumped over the man he'd killed and landed in the winch room. A half dozen of his former colleagues stood with swords, axes, and shields. When they saw Gevere and Kishto, their brows furrowed. Before any of them had the chance to utter the word "traitor," a dozen rioters flooded into the room and ran straight for the guards.

The guard closest to Kishto, a man of middling years called Yuri, came at him with an axe. Kishto took a step back, dodging his blow. Yuri wasn't a fast man, nor was he the smartest. He was also well known for killing prostitutes, and it was that thought that drove Kishto's counter blow, aimed at Yuri's neck. He half-deflected it, the edge of Kishto's blade cutting into his arm. The axe fell from his hand, and Kishto seized the chance to plunge his sword through his leather armour and deep into his gut.

Yuri down, Kishto took a look around the room. Scores of rioters were also down. Blood spurted into the air from wounds and painted the walls and slickened the floorboards. Shouting, grunting, screaming all filled his ears. He could barely hear the guard wailing at him as he jumped

66

forward with a sword, aiming for Kishto's neck. Kishto brought up his blade just in time and realised who he was facing—Bakor's cousin. A young man named Alebe, with dark, intense eyes that carried an untameable wildness. And they looked all the wilder now as he swung his blood-stained sword again. Kishto fell backwards with each parry, losing strength and momentum against his younger, stronger foe. *Just block the blows and wait for your moment*, he told himself, but they kept coming. Alebe feinted, spun his wrist, and slashed Kishto's leg, a deep gash that sent blood spattering across the wooden boards. Another blow followed, the tip of Alebe's sword slicing his chest. Kishto didn't cry out, but a wave of weakness took him. His wounded leg stung and buckled under pressure, but he managed to push himself backwards as Alebe came at him again. Alebe cut air, lost his balance on a pool of blood, and slipped forward onto one knee. Kishto wasted no time. He planted his blade into the gap between neck and shoulder, sinking it a good foot into the other man's body before sliding it out.

Kishto looked around him. He saw nothing but crimson and the pink of offal and gore. Gevere still fought, though his sword was now in his offhand. His other arm hung limp at his side, blood dripping down his fingers. He parried a blow, but his enemy followed up with a brutal slice to the back of the leg. Gevere hit the ground with a groan.

Two more guards wrestled with some of the remaining rioters before kicking them to the ground and stabbing them. The lack of armour and weapons proved telling despite their superior numbers. But all was not yet lost, not while he still stood.

Kishto made his move. He hamstrung one guard who was stabbing a downed protestor, moved past him, and severed the sword arm of the other who was in mid-swing with his axe. With the pair's screams rattling around his helmet, he hurried to Gevere. Kishto shoulder-barged the guard who was about to finish Gevere off—a heifer of a man called Juniper. Kishto didn't let him turn, swinging his sword at him, but Juniper saw it coming, stayed low, and strafed. He brought up his own sword, and Kishto met it. The clang sent his ears ringing. Fighting the shockwave racing up his arm, he tried to move back, but Juniper was on him like a cat with a mouse. The tip of Juniper's sword sliced his off-hand arm. Warm blood flowed down it and dripped from Kishto's fingers. Juniper laughed. He swung again. Kishto parried, but Juniper twisted his wrist and cut a gash along the outside of his forearm. He followed it up with a kick to the gut, knocking Kishto to the ground. He dropped his sword.

"Didn't put you down for a traitorous fuck, Kishto. You always were a bit weak. The gut of a coddled princess, we all say. Always shitting yourself about something. I'm glad I'm the one to finally put you down."

Juniper raised his sword, point aiming for the heart.

"Aghh!"

The sword point changed direction.

Juniper, arms flailing, spun toward the source of his sudden pain— Gevere, on the ground with a dagger, stabbing at his leg over and over. Pained cries melded with the rageful. Juniper hacked down at Gevere, unable, unwilling to stop.

Kishto got to his feet. He yanked Gevere's dagger from Juniper's leg, grabbed the guard's forehead, and ran the blade across his neck. He pushed him aside and looked down at Gevere—unrecognisable now.

Kishto fought pain, rising bile, and intense dizziness. He spat blood and took in the room. The stone walls were painted crimson, so too the ceiling, the floorboards, and the winch that stood in the centre of the room—the reason for all this death. It seemed senseless, meaningless. But to think that would do the lives of these men and women a disservice. They had died fighting for a cause they believed in, one that Kishto had come to believe in. He had to see the job done, for their sakes.

A trio of protestors, lying on the ground, groaned from their wounds.

"Help me turn this if you can," Kishto said, staggering toward the winch, trying not to think about his injuries. One of the protestors got to her feet, a red-haired woman with a gash across her thigh. Kishto put everything he had into the push, shouting to fight his pain and nausea. Straining, the woman cried out too. The winch shifted, gained momentum, and clunked into action.

Cheers from outside came to his ears. Kishto peered through the holes in the ground through which the chains ran and saw a river of bodies hurrying through. Zia had gotten the gate open.

We've done it.

Light-headedness took Kishto. He dropped to the ground next to Gevere. Scores had died, good and bad, just to get to this point, people like Gevere who had given everything for this cause. But was it enough?

Kishto's chest tightened, his vision dimmed. But his pain eased and he felt warm, as if he was in bed, back home safe with his mother, father, and sister. The images of them shifted into the baker and his family. Wounds gaped at their necks and their dead eyes watched as Kishto's final breath escaped his mouth.

The General

Explosions rumbled in the distance. Burning buildings crumbled and fell. Black smoke and grey dust clouds plumed high into the evening sky. Looking out the narrow window of his study, Leo could smell the acrid smoke that poisoned the air. Memories of battlefields stirred in his mind— the charred bodies, singed hair and flesh. A lump formed in his throat. Memories like that had killed his stomach for war, a repulsion that had stayed with him for decades, but it was a secret he would take to the grave. What would the world think of a war hero who had no appetite for fighting, who was afraid of the very notion? Or at least until recently.

Months spent planning had built to this moment. Now was the time to see the fruits of all of their labours. He listened for a good minute before opening his office door. The south tower of the keep would be quietest, he judged, and from there, he could see most of what was happening in the city below. But the keep was crawling with Canterbury's mercenaries—men beyond Leo's military jurisdiction. Get caught by them, and he risked something more painful than a reprimand.

But Leo was a man renewed, his confidence restored, and he was prepared for the potential consequences if things went wrong. The perpetual dull aches in his knees and back had faded—he even felt able to walk without his stick, though he didn't quite trust his balance without it. His mind felt less foggy too. It was Tillia who'd given him this new lease of life. A chance meeting at Lord Howth's ball was the beginning. He'd never seen someone so beautiful look so sad. When he saw the man at her arm, he understood why. And then the cogs of his old mind clicked into gear. He knew her. Her father, Tymas, had made some of the finest swords Leo had ever seen or wielded. Tillia had been a little girl back then. At the ball, they'd spoken about her father, who'd died not long ago in a fire. An accident, her husband Vaso had said. He was a foul-tempered captain of the guards, and close to Canterbury.

For a good few hours, they reminisced, of the weapons her pa made, of times before that fighting in the war, the feats they achieved, the sights they saw—stories a father would never tell his little girl. Tillia had clung to his every word. A few days later, she sought him out and they'd spoken more of the past. Her questions had been thoughtful, and she extracted snippets and pieces of the puzzle without him realising at the time. Several more meetings passed before she revealed her proposal. Leo's heart fluttered as she spoke with passion and enthusiasm about hope and change, about the injustices that pervaded society and how to right them. But to succeed, she needed his help—or the military's, or at least those who could be trusted within the organisation. Leo had chosen it as his final mission. For too long he had felt powerless and weak as Canterbury forced him to the fringes, as evil wrapped its tentacles around the city he loved, the city he had killed and nearly died for. It was torturous to sit on his hands and bite his tongue while his people suffered. He'd needed someone to help him, though. Now, he had a chance to make up for those idle years.

Up the steps of the south tower Leo climbed, his sturdy mahogany walking stick aiding him. He wished he was the tall, broad, and fearsome man he'd been in his youth so he could join the fight today too. With flowing brown hair and a beard to match, women had loved him, but he couldn't care less about their attention. His heart was aligned with one man alone: Lukesh. For years, they had spent every moment together, Lukesh being an officer in the army, Leo his senior commander. Some fools questioned it, but what harm had it done? They'd never lost a battle. His men fought with love in their hearts as well as fire and aggression. There was nothing more powerful.

But good things tend not to last forever. Lukesh died in battle. Leo cut his way through a dozen men to save him, but it was in vain. That failure still weighed heavy in his heart, even now, at the age of eighty-three springs old. He thought he was beyond redemption, unable to make up for his failings, but today he hoped to shift the scales a little more to the centre, to the elusive point of balance in his lifelong struggle between right and wrong.

Leo reached the top level. He paused to take deep breaths and ease his light-headedness. He listened out for anybody who could be beyond the stairwell door. He inched forward, broadening his view into the chamber. Clear. The ladder to the roof was propped in position, and the hatch door closed. A plate of cheese and bread sat on the room's only table. A half-full cup of what smelled like mead stood next to it. His eyes turned to the hatch, weighing the odds of someone being up there. Leo crossed the room to the ladder, tested its sturdiness, and began to climb—a slow and steady pace, but a quiet one. He inched the hatch open, peered through the gap for any feet. Nothing. Exhaling with relief, Leo climbed up onto the tower roof. A gust swept over him, and he had to steady himself with his stick. The stench of charred wood was as strong as the wind itself.

Leo shuffled toward the wall, placing a hand on the cold stone parapet. From up here, he could see the upper part of the city, home to the ruling classes and rich-born. A curtain wall surrounded them and the city beyond. Towers of smoke rose from that part of the city. At the edge of his failing vision, he spied commotion along the wall; what, exactly, he couldn't quite tell. There was more activity between the keep and the wall, where blockades were being hastily assembled by guards along the streets. They were crude constructions, made up of expensive furniture hauled from the grandiose villas and apartments of Pietalos's elite. Some residents had been evacuated. A reckoning lay in store for those who remained. They were holed up here in the keep, unable, unwilling, or perhaps unconcerned that their lives and societal positions were under threat of fundamental change.

The corruption in this city had spread for years. Leo could even pinpoint the moment in time it began—when Canterbury arrived. The snake of a man had appeared one day in Parliament as an advisor to a serving member—some no-mark Leo couldn't remember the name of—and was now chief advisor and main enforcer of the Leader of the House. He was, in effect, the controlling figure in Parliament, the shadow looming over them all. The Leader, a man named Pyotr Garfeld, was a mere stooge and more easily manipulated than a cheating husband caught in the act. Under Canterbury's influence, a series of baffling and damaging decisions had been made: Cutting the rights of workers and empowering the businesses they worked for to do as they please. Giving the city guards free rein to do whatever they wanted to maintain order. Failing to invest any funds in maintaining the poorer parts of the city, allowing disease to spread, homelessness to spike, buildings to crumble and collapse, deaths to rise.

Leo had lobbied hard for an intervention, but received nothing but the door in his face. Under Canterbury and Garfeld, huge swathes of the city's population had become isolated and forgotten, cast aside and left to rot. And to keep them where they were, the two men had sown discord between the people. The creation of the so-called Fight Against Root, or "Uproot the Root," as the campaign slogan went, was an attempt to tackle the growing drug problem in the city. Instead, it served as a means to create a divide amongst the population, an *us and them* mentality. Canterbury peddled the line that it was the fault of the root smokers that there were no jobs. What business would want to set up shop here? It was the rooties' fault that food prices were high. They were stealing it from hard-working people, creating a shortage. It was the rooties' fault that crime was high, that murders and attacks were daily occurrences, rapes and sexual assaults commonplace. It was them committing those crimes in their demented states, desperate for their next fix. When people heard the same thing over and over, at some point, they came to hear it as truth, especially when, in their despair, they sought answers for why their lives were so shit.

A great crack and bang split the air. Beyond the walls in the city below, a ball of fire sparked to life. It grew taller than the tower blocks surrounding the factory district, the area in which it originated. Leo could feel the rumble through the stone as buildings toppled and fell and others became consumed by the expanding fireball. The persistent din of voices, shouts, drums, and fighting took on a frenzied state. Leo grimaced as he watched. His heart ached with guilt. This was the outcome he had feared, that he, no doubt naively, thought they could avoid. Tears came to his eyes. Leo had spent a lifetime doing things he never wanted to do, that he opposed on a moral level. But choice had been taken from him—or had it? That was what he told himself, that the military took away his freedom. But today proved him a fraud—he was going against orders, finally doing what he saw was right.

It pained Leo to watch the breakdown of society. Any sense of community that had existed when he was a child had long been ground into the dirt and detritus that clung to the streets of the city. Day-to-day life for many people was a struggle, a battle to find food, clean water, and to stay out of the way of the wrong people. The streets were dark and lawless, and in the areas close to the Great River, those streets and homes often flooded. People lost everything overnight. It left them living in squalor, and for many, the only way to survive meant turning to a life of depravity. The city had grown into a monster. And the harsh reality was that he was part of the organisation in charge of rearing that monster. Yes, he'd tried to stop things, tried to intervene, but all it had done was whittle away his authority, diminished his role. Canterbury had control, and those failed attempts only saw Leo pushed further and further to the periphery. But still, he was close enough to know what was going on, to know what their weaknesses were. Now he wanted to see if he'd been successful in exploiting them.

Their plan was simple enough—ensure that the rioters and the armed forces they had amassed made it through the gates to the upper part of the city and to the keep. That was where the real battle would take place—Canterbury had a professional force of mercenaries from lands far-flung guarding it. Those mercenaries unnerved Leo. They didn't say much, just nodded and took orders like hounds. All of them had the look of a killer in their eyes. Not just a look that said they'd killed, but that they'd enjoyed it and longed for the moment they got to do so again.

It was a small force of just under two thousand, but well-armed and equipped, and with the benefit of a stout keep, they could tear up a mass of untrained civilians. But Leo had a few surprises in store for them, namely scores of his most loyal and fiercest fighters hidden within the keep, its outbuildings, and the curtain wall, ready to strike when the moment was right. And among the ranks of the protestors were a few thousand military men, loyal to the cause. Many of them were veterans, perhaps too old to fight in some cases. But clad an able man in metal, and regardless of age, he could still do damage.

They had decided to try and take the city swiftly, ride the wave of momentum that had built throughout the day, and try to cut the head off the beast instead of inflicting a few wounds and waiting for it to bleed out. It also deprived Canterbury of the opportunity to call in military reinforcements. Though Leo was most senior of all generals, he'd been removed as chief officer and replaced by a flunky named Mykos Devere. However, he still had some operational control, and in preparation for today, he'd organised large-scale military drills to take place. The whole army had mobilised and marched a week to the south to the Plains of Abera. Twenty thousand soldiers moved slowly. It'd be a while till they got back.

Leo's eyes weren't what they used to be, so he used a looking glass to observe the wall and gates. No sign of movement yet. At the northern gate, black smoke rose from the gatehouse. Either the rioters had started a fire at the base of the wall or, and the likeliest option, the defenders had used burning-hot pitch and oil. Leo had fought in many a siege; he knew the damage pitch and oil could do, especially to groups packed shoulder to shoulder.

"Any sign of them?"

The familiar voice put Leo's ageing heart under a siege of its own.

He turned, expecting to see Canterbury with his flowing brown hair and mocking eyes and smile. Instead, someone or something else stood there, a being who looked altogether harrowing. He wore a muted black robe that swept the stone slabs beneath his feet. And he was tall, on the skeletal side of thin, with narrow shoulders and a neck that looked too small to support his large, egg-like head. A few wispy strands of hair clung to it, and his cheeks and chin were bare. Heavy bags sagged beneath dark eyes as if he had never known sleep, like two craters on the face of the moon.

"Who in Tervia are you?" Leo said.

The figure smiled. "Why, your good friend Canterbury, of course." He gave the slightest of bows. "I look a little different, but that does not matter now." He took a step closer to Leo.

"I found your agents. Very clever, Leo. It took me a while to work out it was you. I didn't think someone so old and fucking useless could muster the energy to pull it off. But here we are, the city aflame and the people you claim to love dying in the thousands because of your dementia-riddled ideologies." His final words carried venom.

"You are the one ordering their deaths. Stand down, admit defeat, and nobody else needs to die," Leo said in a firm tone.

It stirred a broader grin from Canterbury. "Let's not play chicken and egg. It's a waste of time. And you have so little of it left."

"I could say the same for you."

Canterbury chuckled, amusement dancing in his eyes. "They will not pass the keep wall, and like newborn babies thrown against stone, they will all perish, and on your shoulders that will rest."

"Do you fail to see the contradictions in your statements, or is this your game, to propound a false narrative with the conviction of someone guided by truth?"

Canterbury's laughter died but his smile remained. His eyes narrowed a little. "*You* have ordered them to their deaths."

"No, this began when you arrived in Pietalos and started to systematically destroy their lives."

"Destroy lives? Who is this you speak of? It is not me. I have made the lives of these people infinitely better."

"How?" Leo snapped. The temperature rose in his cheeks.

"Dear Leo, you must be going senile, for do you not recall the new sewage system we unveiled just a few years ago?"

It was Leo's turn to laugh. "Aye, and ironically, it's a load of shit. All you've done is pump the waste into the river. There are no fish left in that water. Fishermen have to go out to sea in their river canoes to find something to catch, and many don't return. The water people drink is poison. It's safer to drink mead. With all the shit in the port, the river has silted and ships can't dock. That's meant there are food shortages and prices have gone through the roof. People are losing jobs, getting kicked out of their homes and left on the street with their kids, where your corrupt guards turn them over for petty things like drugs and theft, and then they end up in prison, their lives ended."

Canterbury's thin lips curled into a smile. The sight sparked a flash of anger within Leo and spurred him on.

"What I have come to learn is that this is all by design. You seek to control people's lives from birth to the grave, to limit their freedoms and choices. Is that what you think governance is? The state controlling everything? And what happens when it becomes corrupt? I'll tell you. The people bleed. They get churned up in the cogs of the machine. What you see happening today is what happens when the hand of the state grips the throat of the people too tightly. Back a scared, beaten dog into a corner, and there's always a chance it will lunge and bite, no matter how hard you beat it. Humans are animals, after all."

"It's a pretty picture you paint, General, and no doubt the fools you preach to believe it, but none of it is true. It is all simply the way in which you've framed it. None of it is related. You have drawn those conclusions yourself. Come on, General, be honest with yourself. This city has never been better. These people have yearned for a strong, guiding hand, more so than what any group of wastrel politicians can offer. They need the vision that I have and that they lack, the grit to see it come to life. People don't know what to choose, how best to live their lives. They're all just guessing their way to the grave. They desire leadership and need to be guided in the right ways to think and act."

"That's according to you. What if you're the wrongest person in Tervia? But what does that matter? We're all the hero of our own story."

"Is it not better to write your own story than let another dictate it to you, someone with a lesser mind? And before you answer me, General, tell me what it is you're doing here this very moment. By your definition, you're no different to me."

"Oh, I think I am. We see the world in very different ways."

Canterbury smiled. "But we both see the world differently than them." He pointed to the city. The unsettling-looking man walked over to the parapets and looked out over the fires and chaos. Leo coughed at his scent as he neared—like that of a rotten animal.

"A beautiful sight, no? All that death and destruction. A purge of ugliness and uselessness. It's like unblocking a drain."

Leo had a blade secreted in the handle of his walking stick. He sized up Canterbury. He was taller than Leo by a full head, and who knew what age the pale man was. He looked as thin as Leo, however, and that gave him hope.

"We lead, they follow. More than anyone, you must know the importance of that, General. And no doubt you enjoy it, no?" Leo could feel Canterbury's persuasive ways trying to leech into him.

"Leading through fear and leading through respect are very different things."

Canterbury turned and looked down at him with those cold, dark eyes. "Here you go with the differences again. Fear and respect are means to the same end—control."

"So that's what it's all about, control?"

Canterbury smiled, turned away from him, and again regarded the riotous city. "Even if they do somehow manage to break through the wall of the upper city, by sheer force of will perhaps, they will not survive the blockades along the streets leading to the keep. Plus, I have a surprise for them if they do make it beyond those. And even then, they must overcome the keep's defences and the born killers who hold it. How did you think you could succeed?" Canterbury looked at him, his tone mocking.

"It is no longer a matter of enduring what life has become under your rule. This is their fight for survival. They do not care if they die, for they do not live anyway. That is what you are up against—tens of thousands of angry people who do not care anymore. If I were you, I'd be afraid."

Canterbury laughed like a maniac. "I *am* fear. I devote my life to it. I instil it in others," he shouted.

"Well, if that's the case, you're about as useful as a shield made of butter."

A frown. Leo was getting under his putrid skin.

"Call it off, Leo, and save your *beloved* people."

Leo smiled. "That's not my decision to make. Besides, this is a runaway cart that cannot be stopped."

Canterbury's frown deepened. Gone were the smirks and smiles. Malice and hate filled his eyes. *He think it's just me behind this.*

"Tell me what you know and I will make your end swift."

"I think you should kiss my wrinkly arse. The Master of Whispers, I thought you called yourself. Eyes in every wall, ears in every room, you used to boast. How have you managed to miss the planning of an entire movement against you?"

Canterbury reached inside his cloak and drew a dagger, the blade made of something black—obsidian or metal, Leo couldn't tell which. Leo drew his own blade. It was shorter, but needle-sharp.

"Tell me this, Canterbury. What's the true reason behind you coming here and taking control? Why did you fuck everything up so much?"

"Why do you think, General?"

Leo shrugged, and as he did, they began to circle the roof of the tower. "Control, yes, and much, much more," Canterbury said. "There are forces at work beyond your comprehension, General. The actions we all take matter in the Great Battle beyond. This is my contribution. And after I destroy your pathetic uprising, the real work can begin. And trust me, General, you don't want to be around for that." An involuntary shudder ran down Leo's spine.

"Since we're sharing, tell me—why wait now to rebel? Why sit on your hands for years, watching all this so-called suffering? Why didn't you help sooner?"

"Maybe I should have."

Canterbury scoffed. "Maybe you're a fraud. You claim to hate death, but I can see in your eyes that you'd love nothing more than to kill me. And you're happy to send thousands to their graves today without hesitation. Fraud." He said the final word slowly, as if twisting the verbal blade in Leo's gut.

"I'm not a fraud, but I've spent my life living as one thanks to people like you giving me orders and enforcing them under the guise of honour and bogus laws." For the rest, Leo had no rebuttal. Canterbury was right about another thing too—Leo would love to sink his blade into the ugly bastard.

Canterbury made to strike. Leo braced himself, but he had to fight to keep his eyes on the deformed man as a great crash filled the air. The cheers of thousands of people followed. Leo looked beyond Canterbury, who himself had turned to see what was happening. Off to the east, in the direction of the Servant's Gate, came a wall of sound. A torrent of bodies carrying torches moved up the road toward the keep and right into the blockades that had been set up by the city guards and Canterbury's mercenaries.

"Still feeling brave, Canterbury?"

Canterbury turned and hissed. He leapt at Leo. Age bested the old man more so than his opponent. He tried to grab Canterbury's blade hand but only managed a fistful of his cloak. Leo swung his dagger. Canterbury grabbed his wrist and stopped it. Leo scrambled to get a hold of Canterbury's other arm, but not before the black blade sank into his chest. Pain exploded. He gasped for air but could find none.

"Goodbye, General," Canterbury said. With both hands, he grabbed Leo's jerkin, lifted him up, and threw him off the tower.

Leo watched the stars as he fell. And he smiled, content that he had done the right thing.

The Revolutionary

A heady mix of adrenaline and delight coursed through Till's veins. The torrent of bodies moved through the gatehouse like water through a burst dam, the people cheering and chanting as they went. Help would be coming for the wounded, especially now they'd taken the walls of Upper Town. Others lying on the ground were guards, the ignorant servants of the elite, the embodiment of everything she had come to hate. Though they made the same pleas for mercy, comfort, for the presence of a loved one so they didn't face the void alone, Till held little sympathy for them.

It was intoxicating to see all her plans unfold. Plans that had been a year in the making, that had come close to collapsing on more than one occasion. But with the help of people like Leo and Dhijs, Gerida, Zia and little Mal, they were close to succeeding. Everyone had played their part. Without that, this revolution would not have been possible. Till had vowed to ensure they would each have a stake in the new age to come.

But they still had work to do.

The keep remained intact, and now her warriors and comrades— the people of Pietalos, the beating heart of the city—swept toward it. Her view out of the gatehouse's narrow window limited her scope, but she could see barricades on more than a few streets. Atop them stood archers and crossbowmen, already aiming, waiting for their foes to come into range. More of her people would die here, but she had able fighters leading the assault. They were Leo's men, decorated officers, veterans of war. Their experience would make a monumental difference when it came to organising her ragtag bunch of a few thousand semi-trained volunteers, plus the disaffected citizens who swelled their ranks by tens of thousands—men, women, and no doubt a few children, which Till despaired at, but this was their fight as much as it was hers. Today was a fight for all their futures, for a continuation of life as it was meant nothing but a future of perpetual struggle, of misery, and pain until death became the most desirable option. Some hastened the process through drink, root, or myriad narcotics and potions. She didn't blame them for wanting an escape. She placed that blame on the elite, and for taking advantage of the problem, the pushers and gangs. She had a plan for them, too, one that was being carried out right now. Not only would the city wake up free of corrupt politicians and noblemen and women, but free of the leeches who drained society and took advantage of the wounds of the poor.

It would be a fresh start for all, something Till and the people of this city yearned for. But first she had to do something to liberate herself, to shatter the bondage that had shackled her mind and spirit and come close to killing her. She had to find him. And so far, he was proving to be an elusive bastard. She expected no less of her husband.

Vaso was the definition of a snake. A duplicitous man who bent like paper in a breeze if it suited his ends, which was making money and improving his standing. Serial killers had more of a moral compass than Vaso, who delighted in the beatings and murders he ordered each day as a captain in the city guards.

Till had met Vaso through her father; he'd made Vaso a number of swords over the years. They were all for decoration, of course. Till knew how to dance with a blade—her pa had schooled her ever since she could walk—and Vaso never gave any indication that he could. He was a food-loving, aging manipulator who revelled in pulling strings.

When her pa first started struggling with the pain in his chest, Vaso had begun to show more of an interest in Till. With her big, bright eyes, dark hair, and fair complexion, she drew the eye of many a Low

Town man. But she loathed the mithering attention, the pinch here, a grab there. She'd broken more than a few men's fingers. Back then, Vaso had presented himself as an altogether different man—kind, caring, compassionate, charming, even. He called round with medicine and food, sometimes bringing a healer, always showing genuine concern for her pa. Her pa's dying wish was for her to be cared for after he left, so when Vaso asked his permission for her hand, he was all too enthusiastic about the prospect. "He's a good man with a good heart. He'll look after you," her pa had said. Turned out, he hadn't known shit.

In the depths of her sorrow, she'd agreed to her father's wishes so he could pass without the worry that his daughter was going to starve, get raped, or killed. Vaso had done two of those things; Till was determined not to let him do the latter, that it would be her that did the killing. *Fuck me, does he deserve it.*

For a long time, Till blamed her father for selfishly marrying her off for his peace of mind. She loathed that he felt she was incapable of living her life without a man to protect her. She'd grown up in the heart of Pietalos—she knew the streets and people, and she was more dangerous than most. She expected him to know better, to trust her and think more of her, not just as his little girl. But it was something he wasn't capable of. He was too caring, and by default, too controlling. Till had resolved to let her anger toward him go, to accept him for who he was, good and ill. Nobody was perfect, though they could still hurt and disappoint you. Now, she thought only of the good, happy times, of them cooking and eating together, of them working in the forge, going for trips to the countryside, swimming in the Great River before it became toxic.

Somehow, her pa clung on and made it to Till's wedding, well enough even to hand her over to Vaso. And seeing the joy and relief on her pa's face had made it all worthwhile. Until Vaso took her back to their bedchamber and beat her bloody.

But it wasn't sickness that took her pa in the end. Instead, it was a fire. Awoken in the dead of night by a messenger, she discovered the smithy—her family home—aflame. People tried in vain to douse the flames, but like the furnaces her pa had stoked for decades, they were all-consuming. It'd happened around the time he'd asked her to take over the smithy—she pretty much had already, and Vaso didn't like it. He didn't want his pretty little bride hammering swords all day.

"Your job is to cook and clean and do as I say," he'd said before clipping her round the back of the head.

When Pa died, Vaso was sympathetic, and then came the change. Ice sealed his heart, and his actions against her shifted between beatings, rape, and verbal abuse. She became numb to it all, a walking, hollow corpse. On the day she'd resolved to take her own life, she'd gone back to the smithy as a last goodbye, walked around the husk it now was. Among the rubble and charred remains, she found something—a pin, and one she recognised. It bore the emblem of a gang that plagued much of Low Town and Pietalos. Finding that changed something in her. No longer did she want to end her life. Instead, she wanted to find out who took her father's.

And that's how it began. The first seeds of revolution planted. Of the fight back. And here it now was, unfolding before her, the fruits of her pain and labour.

"Till." Gerida's deep voice rumbled around the chamber. She'd met Gerida through Dhijs, over a year ago now. Tall with midnight-black skin, the one-armed Gerida was the most loyal and dependable man she knew—the only person she could trust for what she was about to do.

"Found him?" Till asked.

She'd given Gerida the task of searching the gatehouse and ramparts for Vaso.

He nodded. "We think so."

"Lead on."

They ran through the bowels of the old city wall, the sounds of fighting, of the dying, hitting them as they passed the narrow windows that punctuated the wall to their left. In the scant light, they saw more than a few dead bodies on the ground, the blood pooling on the stone a threat to a sure foot. The shouts of men and women, of steel clashing and clanging began to echo off the walls. Torchlight burned up ahead. Till's anticipation grew. The moment she had thought about, had dreamed about, had played over time and time again in her mind was nearly here. It set her heart fluttering with excitement and carried her past Gerida and toward the battle.

Till skidded around the corner, blades in hand, and stepped into a chamber. Four of her fellow revolutionaries, faces and bodies wrapped in black, save for their eyes, held their swords up to a single guard, who had dropped his blade in surrender. Half a dozen other guards lay dead on the ground, their blood painting the walls and glistening in the light of the braziers. None of them was Vaso, and neither was the last surviving guard. She sighed and approached him—a pale, ginger-haired man with acne on his blood-smeared face. Fear kept his eyes on the ground, away from his would-be killers and the lifeless corpses who were once his fellow guardsmen.

"Where the fuck is Vaso?" Till asked.

He stuttered the name back in response.

"Yes, Vaso, the ugly cunt of a captain of yours. Where is he? Tell me and live."

For the first time, he looked up, still afraid. Till pulled down the scarf covering her face.

"Please, tell me." She looked into his hazelnut eyes. His grimace eased, eyes locked on hers. She had him.

"He's running for the keep with a bunch of officers. They said they were going down Myrtel Street."

"Thank you. You can join us and fight or stay out of the way. Choice is yours." She turned to the four revolutionaries and Gerida, who

86

loomed tall behind them. "Let's go." She turned back before they left and saw the guard sink to his knees, sobbing. Till suspected he wouldn't be moving for a while; his soiled breeches wouldn't comfortably take him far.

It almost felt fitting that she found herself heading back to Myrtel Street. It was there Vaso had paraded her around at a ball in some rich-born's manse a few years back. One of the worst nights of her life. That pretentious dick-swinging display, followed by Vaso raping her when they got home. For a long time after, she had lived in the deepest pit of despair, a bleakness akin to living in a world where the sun never rose, with no hope that it ever would. Somehow, she escaped that place. Never did she want to return.

After descending the wall's steps, they made their way along the cobbled streets of Upper Town, past great oak trees with spring leaves bursting out upon their branches and well-manicured lawns that ran in strips along the centre of the street. For some, it was the first time they'd seen something alive and green that wasn't a weed in the stone jungle of Lower Town. Grand buildings, three or four storeys high, stood shoulder to shoulder opposite the wall. This had been the city's original boundary before Pietalos swelled to a size no city planner could have foreseen. Over the centuries, plague, famine, and war had driven people from rural areas to the city, where they hoped they'd find some help and support. They'd have gotten more from a pack of wolves.

The old wall served the elite well in keeping out the malodorous rabble. But now it had been breached, and thousands of her fellow citizens moved along streets they'd never trampled before. Myrtel Street was the furthest west, and soon she and Gerida cut onto it and found a dense river of people marching forward. Some bore torches, others makeshift weapons in the form of sticks, poles, pitchforks, blacksmith hammers, farming implements like scythes and flails. "Get them out!" was the universal chant, referring to the politicians and elite holed up in the keep. Till joined in for a couple of verses.

She hopped onto a water barrel beside a hitching post and looked over the mass of heads. Further down the street, she saw a mound of what looked like furniture—tables, chairs, bookcases, stuff hauled from the plush houses and apartments around them. It all served to form a blockade right across the street, high enough to slow a person down and force them to climb in order to pass. Time enough for the defenders to cut them down or pick them off with a few darts. A big, sustained charge might overcome it. *It can't be that solid*, she judged. Those protestors at the front of the group stopped not far from the blockade, as if debating their next move. "Charge!" Till shouted at the top of her lungs to urge them on. Gerida picked up the cry. But there was too much noise, too many people chanting protest lines. Till thought about trying to fight her way to the front, but there were hundreds blocking her way there.

Upon the blockade, helmeted heads appeared, so too the tips of longbows. They climbed higher, a long line of archers and crossbowmen emerging. As one, they raised their weapons and shot in a well-timed volley. Every dart, it seemed, found a target, cleaving a swathe of protestors. Panic exploded. Some up for the fight charged at long last. Others fled, and some collided with each other, the press too thick for escape. Only a smattering of people reached the blockade, a fractured advance put down with ease by the archers. A few hurled rocks and torches, but they bounced off the cobbles or wooden blockade. One or two suffered hole-punching bolts to the body in response, and more death-dealing volleys followed, escalating the panic further. Till hopped off her barrel just as someone was shoved into it, knocking it over and sending gallons of water everywhere.

"This is fucked," Till said to Gerida, the pair of them up against a wall at the side of the street, out of the way of the chaos. "We need to get past this blockade."

"What're you thinking?" Gerida said.

Till scanned the apartments and houses flanking the road. "The balconies, maybe?"

"We'd end up with a dart in our back or arse," Gerida said, typically deadpan.

"If we're fast, we might not."

Gerida looked around. "Don't see any better choices."

"Come on, let's try and get closer."

They kept their shoulders to the fancy apartments, taking shoves from panicking protestors as they moved. Arrows dropped indiscriminately from the fire-lit sky, those on the barricade now shooting at will. People dropped, the bodies piling atop each other as arrows pierced flesh and bone. A few brave people still tried to charge at the guards, but they were taken out before they got close enough to attack.

Keeping low, Till and Gerida hurried up a short set of steps leading to an apartment block close to the makeshift barricade. Gerida burst through the door with a firm shoulder and they found themselves in a dim hallway. The chaotic noises quietened as they made their way up a grand marble stairway, heading for the highest level.

Gerida slowed to a stop on the top landing. The weak glow of fires outside filtered in through a window at the opposite end, overlooking Myrtel Street. A few panes had been smashed, broken glass glittering on the ground. Between here and there stood three doors, two on the right, one on the left; leading to apartments, she guessed. Gerida wasted no time kicking in the one on the right, closest to the window. Pained screams and pleas for help echoed up from below. The protestors had retreated to a point the arrows could not reach. They hurled insults and rocks and bricks, none of them in any danger of hitting a target. But it kept the fight alive, and for that, Till was proud and grateful.

The apartment was deserted. Vast walls bore gold-rimmed paintings of people Till couldn't give a shit about, as well as elegant tapestries depicting scenes from the city's past, like grand battles her father no doubt fought in. *Will they make a tapestry about today?*

A cold hearth big enough to roast a well-aged boar dominated the wall on their right, and opposite stood a series of tall windows, one of which had doors leading to a balcony. They crept toward it and peered outside.

The barricade stood below, out of the eyeline of the guards, though Till was convinced the guards would see them as soon as they started moving. The next balcony over was way too far to jump to, and there was no ledge to shimmy along. The hope of that plan coming to fruition took an arrow to the heart like so many of her comrades on the street below. But her hope didn't flee. The balcony boasted a well-kept garden, complete with a leaf-covered trellis that stretched upwards, though how far, she couldn't quite see. But it might be high enough to allow them to climb onto the roof. She inched open the door, grateful for the potted shrubs that provided some cover. A glance up revealed a trellis affixed to the wall, leading all the way to the roof. She grabbed the frame, tried to shake it. Solid. She gave Gerida a nod.

A voice within told her to hurry, to get up and out of the way before anyone could look up. But speed wasn't possible. She looked back down to see Gerida making his first moves. Having just the one arm put him at a huge disadvantage. Shield on his back, he used his stump as best he could, but the trellis beams weren't thick enough to get any purchase with. He even used his teeth, biting onto the wisteria's branches. Till gave him a hand, but the man was so heavy she could do little beyond offering him some balance. They made good progress, though, and the slate was in touching distance when the trellis beam Gerida stood upon snapped. He jolted downwards, sending leaves into the air and to the street below. Till grabbed his leathers and pulled with everything she had.

"I'm good," Gerida said, and Till's pounding heart eased for all but a second. Shouts erupted from ground level.

"Go!" Gerida roared.

No sooner had the word left his mouth did the first arrow smack into the wall beside her, shattering the painted plaster. More followed in a barrage, but they were shots taken with haste.

Till hauled herself up the last stretch and got her feet onto the roof, though the slate tiles wobbled and clanked whenever she moved. More arrows began to fly at them. Till reached out for Gerida, got a hold of his wrist. An arrow whizzed over her head. Ducking between her shoulders, she hauled her friend up the last stretch and away from the roof's edge. They scrambled to a flatter part, where huge chimney stacks rose towards the sky. Against the brick of one, she rested, catching her breath, her eyes on the unfolding carnage around them. Here she had the best view yet of what they had achieved, and the destruction created by both sides. Behind them, down the hill towards the Great River, swathes of the city burned. Factories and warehouses, apartment blocks, houses, shops. People's possessions. Their memories. She told herself that most of them had nothing, that what would rise from the ashes would be better for all. But now, looking at those flames, smelling charred flesh and wood and hearing panic and fear and pain, the cold blade of doubt pressed itself against her neck, hard enough to draw blood. She had contributed to this. People had died because of her. Could she really justify the means to the end?

Yes. This was Canterbury's and his minions' fault. Nobody else's.

While the fighting and killing had simmered on Myrtel Street, the revolutionaries were on the barricade on the next street over, battling hand to hand. *And winning, I hope.* No doubt more battles like it were unfolding all across Upper Town. This had been their target, the centre of corruption and elitism in the city, the place where the lives of those further down the hill were toyed with like pieces in a game. The anger that thought triggered dispelled her doubt. Now the rules of the game had changed.

Off in the far distance, she could see their final goal—the Old Keep, the place where the People's Parliament gathered, and the source of corruption. She wondered whether Vaso was in there too. It didn't matter where he hid; Till would find him. It was the one thing she'd promised herself this morning when she woke, before she went to meet Dhijs. That seemed like a different age now.

Gerida prompted her to move, and she realised she'd let her mind wander.

"This far enough?" Gerida asked after they'd scrambled across the roof tiles.

"It should do."

"How we gettin' down? 'Cos I don't fancy climbing again."

"Through the roof?"

Gerida looked down at the slates, appearing unconvinced. Till bent down, and with a bit of a wobble, yanked a tile free. "My pa had a roofer friend who used to buy iron nails from him. Said loads of cheap bastards would never pay for nails for the slates. The people in Upper Town were the worst, he said. Looks like we're in luck."

They pulled free a bunch of tiles and climbed down into an attic space. A hatch at the end of the attic led down to a grand bedroom, the drop a little higher than Till would have liked, the connection with the floor sending a shockwave through her ankles. After a few moments of pain, it passed. Gerida's drop was even heavier, but he, too, seemed unharmed. A twisted or broken ankle at this stage would be devastating.

A quick glance out the window confirmed they were behind the barricade. Till's heart froze. Her eyes were drawn to one figure among the rabble. Long black cloak draped over broad shoulders. Hair that was once bleach-blond, now grey, his neat beard the same shade. Vaso was a man who stood out from the crowd, she would grant him that. But for Till, it wasn't for the right reasons. While his fair colouring might turn heads, his leering eyes held an intense, eager look. In public, he was the man Till had known at first—the perfect charmer. In private, he was different, the shift dramatic. He lived life like a game of charades, changing his face when it suited him to mask his calculating ruthlessness. That was the side she saw most of, the one that had come close to breaking her, and the one she was determined to destroy.

Vaso spoke with a bunch of pikemen, giving instructions and orders before he set off down the street, away from the barricade and toward the keep, flanked by two guards. Till's instinct was to follow, but they still had the task of breaking down that barricade. Those archers were killing her people, revelling in every heart they stilled. They had to pay, but Till wasn't quite sure how to deal with so many. Taking out Vaso, however, was more achievable. And something she yearned for with every fibre of her being.

"Let's go," Till said, taking the lead. Gerida followed without question. She'd never known anyone to trust her as much as he did, and she was glad he was with her now. As much as she hated Vaso, his hooks still sank deep into her soul, tainting her thoughts with fear. Gerida would help her see the job done—if she needed it.

They moved through the apartment, into the communal hallway, and began to descend the main steps of the grand building. She drew both her shortswords. Gerida shifted his grip on his axe and flexed his shield arm. The round shield was heavy, too heavy for Till—she'd never felt comfortable using one. A sword in each hand suited her best. Perfect balance. She'd practised this way since she was old enough to run and jump. Her pa, one of the finest swordsmen in the Pietalos army, had schooled her well. Till had inherited her father's swiftness of hand and that extra sense needed in those desperate moments, the ability to breathe when others panicked, to almost slow the pace of time and see things with clarity. It was a skill untested until she became "Shadow." Soon after that, she discovered just how much better she was than most people in those life-and-death moments. And she learned another thing about herself—killing didn't weigh heavy on her conscience. It was a realisation she'd come to after she'd heard a woman getting raped. She found the perpetrator to be a guard. Triggered by the abuse Vaso had dealt her, she'd stabbed the guard in the back, over and over, and found it… satisfying. It flooded her with a sense of power at a time when she felt powerless, made her feel in control when she felt like she had none.

Those who fell to her swords did so in pursuit of her cause, a cause that belonged to the people of Pietalos. It was just like a war, and her pa had always said killing in wars was different than killing during times of peace. When she'd put that to Dhijs, she got an earful about how all killing was the same, that to take the life of another was the ultimate sin, regardless of the justification. Till got it, but she grew annoyed with Dhijs's refusal to see her side of the argument. Killing a corrupt, murdering rapist was different than killing a young child innocent of any wrong. As much as it frustrated her, she knew the importance of his puritan mind. Checks and balances like this were necessary. More than once, her anger had gotten the better of her, and that led to errors, as she'd learned the first time she hit a gang's stash house. She'd been brave and drunk on bloodlust and thought she could take the reinforcements that came to the gang's aid. A desperate chase ensued, and two of her people had died. Mistakes today would cost them, and they could afford none for this to work.

As they reached the bottom of the stairs, the front doors burst open. In poured a gang of guards armed with shields and spears, their conical helms looking more like the heads of cocks than those of soldiers. Their dirty yellow tabards said everything about their organisation—corrupt and puss-rotten to the core, her husband at the heart of it, if not the beating muscle himself. Their spears fell with murderous intent as they charged across the stretch of open marble floor.

"First proper fight today," Till said.

"I've been looking forward to it," Gerida replied. With a grin, he charged, too, and Till followed.

She locked eyes on a stout man, closer than the others, and marked the two behind him. She ran at him, full pelt. His charge grew wilder, as though he fancied his odds. Ten paces away, Till dropped and slid across the slick marble. The spearpoint lashed out like a striking snake. The point caught her black cloak, and she heard a rip. But she was behind her enemy now, and she slashed with both blades, severing his hamstrings. She rolled to her feet as he fell to the ground, dodging the spearheads that clanked off the stone. Till pressed the enemy to her right, a rotund man who tried to bash her with his shield. She moved left, spun past the shield, and sunk her left sword deep into his side. She pushed him into his comrade with her foot, freeing her blade. She didn't give him a chance to settle, arcing a high slash at his phallic helm. He blocked it with his shield, but it blew open his guard. Till sank her other blade through his chest.

Gerida had dispatched his foes too. Blood smearing the side of his face, he gave her a nod and led on out the doors and onto the street. The smell of fire was thick in the air, an unending din of shouting and screaming echoing along the street. To their left was the blockade. But they headed right, after Vaso.

"I've never asked 'cos it ain't my business, but what are you going to do to this bastard when you get him?"

"Something I've thought long and hard about. I can think of no better end than what I have planned for the man who took everything from me."

Behind enemy lines, the street was clear. They weren't too far from the keep now, and no doubt that was where Vaso was headed, scurrying away to the safety of his rat hole. If they let him get beyond the walls, she might never catch him. Till couldn't shake the feeling that her chance was slipping away.

The road bent to the right, and there, in the distance, she saw him. She could recognise that limp and pale bouffant hair a mile off. He was a good way ahead, but they had eyes on him, and seeing him this close filled her with a rush of fire and fury. She hurtled down the cobbled street.

Vaso and his two guardsmen turned. She was close enough to see her husband's eyes widen. He took off and disappeared down a path to the left. The two guards drew their swords and held their ground.

"You get Vaso, I'll put these down," Gerida said. Till loved him at that moment. Gerida slowed as they approached the two guards, but Till continued at a sprint. Uttering a roar, she hopped and slashed, aiming a brace of fierce blows at one of the guards. The first blow deflected off his sword and the second his helm, knocking it off and stunning the man.

Till didn't look back as she passed them, eyes on the spot she last saw Vaso. She followed the path he'd disappeared down—a gravelled trail through a manicured lawn, with other trails leading off it to townhouses. Oak trees grew tall and darkened the night further. She tried to put herself in his sadistic head. It wasn't hard to work out what he'd do. *Hide.*

Blade in each hand, Till crept among the shadows as she loved to do. Safe, where no one could see her, but she could see them. Up ahead, a puddle glistened in the moonlight, the edge of a fresh print in the mud next to it. More prints followed it, heading left along a pathway that led to the rear entrance of a townhouse. She approached the door, mindful not to make noise, when the leaves of a tree rustled to the left. She spun, swords raised, ready to strike. A magpie stared at her from a branch. It tilted its head, flicked its long tail, then flew off to a nearby building. Till frowned and brought her attention back to the task at hand.

She found the door open, the lock splintered and broken. She peered inside first, wary of an ambush. It was the kind of cheap move he'd try to make. Anything to survive. She took a quiet step inside, the battle in the streets falling to a din. She caught a whiff of sweat and body odour, mixed with sweet spices and cloves. Vaso wasn't one for regular washing. His skid-ridden undergarments that she had to wash were evidence enough of that. In an attempt to mask it, he wore expensive scents and perfumes, which combined to make him smell even more foul.

Till followed the smell, finding herself in a corridor, a stairway leading upstairs to her right. All her senses were heightened now. She was like a mountain lion closing in on its prey, stalking through the brush, waiting for the moment to pounce.

Till looked around the two rooms on either side of the stairs and found nothing but grandiose and uncomfortable furniture and bawdy portraits of ugly rich people sitting in poses that would make you think they'd conquered the world. That left upstairs. She crept up each step; it was a testament to the money spent on this place that the boards didn't creak. It made her job a lot easier. At the top of the stairs, she caught that pungent smell of cloves again, and it led her to a room at the far end of the landing. The door was closed over, not shut. Heart racing with anticipation, she pushed it the rest of the way open. Vaso stood tall at the far end of the room, holding a sword with a confident firmness. But his eyes told a different picture. He was uncertain, afraid. Seeing it spurred Till on. She stepped inside and closed the door behind her. For a long while, she looked at him, and he at her.

"You're Shadow?" he asked at last.

With her face covered by her scarf and with the hood up, he didn't recognise her. She nodded.

"You've caused me quite a few headaches this past year. It's nice to meet you in the flesh. But not as nice as having your head on a spike." He flexed his sword arm in what she knew was meant to be a threatening way. "So, what do you want?" His voice wavered a touch. A bead of sweat ran down the side of his face.

A hidden smile stretched across Till's face. Now was the time. She pulled down her hood and scarf. It was a moment she had dreamed of for a long time, revealing herself to him before she served him justice. Her smile grew as his eyes widened. She could see in his eyes the rush of questions flooding his mind, could see the fear swell like a tumour.

"Why are you here?" Vaso stammered.

"Why do you think?" She held her swords up as if pointing out the obvious. "To kill you."

She took a step forward to see what he'd do. He brought up his sword in defence.

"Tillia, darling, there's no need for any of this. Whatever your reasoning, I'm sure it's just a misunderstanding."

"I'm sure it's not," she said, her tone firm.

Vaso frowned at the rebuttal. "I've never harmed a woman before, and I do not wish to now."

Till couldn't hold in her laugh. "Does your wife not count? Am I mere property to you? I'm sure you've hurt plenty besides me. Killed a few, too, I'm sure. I know you well enough to see when you're playing your classic victim card. Always trying to manipulate emotions, aren't you? Strumming away on the heart strings." She spun her wrists, the blades rotating. "Do you remember the time I came to you about one of your guards raping a woman in an alley? Do you remember what you said?"

He shook his head.

"'She was probably asking for it.' What woman do you know has ever asked to be raped? Did I ever ask you for it the countless times you've done it?"

He scoffed at that.

"A husband can't rape his wife, is that it? When I say no and you do it anyway, that's rape. That's all you are—a rapist pig, no better than the piece of shit who raped that woman. Do you know what I did to him? I killed him, and he squealed like the pig he was. What made that feel even better was seeing how angry you were when you heard a guard was found dead with his pants around his ankles. The rats had made a good go of his cock, hadn't they? Not that there was much to go at."

Till laughed, and her husband squirmed. "I got to liking that feeling of seeing you suffer, even chased it. I'd wake each morning with a smile, knowing you had to deal with the shit I'd left for you overnight."

"If what you say is true, you've killed scores of people. You question my morals while you stand there as a mass murderer," he said.

"If that's what you call me, how do you describe yourself? All of that vigilantism didn't cut it in the end, anyway. The corruption in this city runs deep, and I'm grateful to you for opening my eyes at those boring, pompous balls the rich-born love so much. Taking out a few of your politician friends still wasn't enough, though. You nearly lost your job because of them, which was hilarious. But I realised the system had to be torched, and certain individuals had to be removed, like you and your good friend Canterbury. Luckily, General Leo is of the same mindset as me. He was all too happy to take this to the next level. And here we are. I can't tell you how long I've waited for this moment, to finally kill you and rid you from my life.

"You see, Vaso, I know what you did to my pa. Who started that fire. Who paid them to start it. You're no good at covering your tracks. Did you get a bit spooked when that pusher gang you hired all turned up dead? Did you think someone was coming for you too? Did you get *scared*, Vaso? Is that why we had those guards outside our house all those months? Little did you know, you were in bed with the killer." She laughed in delight. "I just love how you think you're so cunning and deceptive. A real puppeteer. But you're as competent as the rooties you prey on each day." Her tone was mocking, words hacking him to pieces. His cheeks were the shade of red wine. The anger was building, just like she wanted.

"All I want to know is why. Why did you kill my pa? You already had me bound and chained and he was dying. What threat could he have been? Or was it because you didn't want your wife running a smithy? Not ladylike enough for you?"

He didn't answer, but his eyes narrowed and his brows furrowed. Till had never seen the man apologise for anything. It wasn't in his makeup. She wasn't expecting anything like that here, but this was all part of the end he deserved, to make him suffer and squirm, to let this manipulative prick know that the one person he thought he controlled the most was undermining him the entire time.

"I don't understand why you obsess so much over your father's death. Look at what the man has driven you to. Is this really what you want for yourself in life? To be this paranoid, insecure hag of a woman?"

Till couldn't help put laugh. "Me insecure? One thing I've realised about you is that you're the very definition of insecurity. Do you rape your wife to prove to yourself you're not some weak, insignificant wastrel? Or do you do it because you like to feel the power of control? Your insecurities aren't just a problem for you; they've become a problem for thousands of people in this city. You're part of the corruption that has devoured any sense of good, and you need to be torn out and reduced to ashes."

She took another step closer.

Anger flashed in his eyes, nostrils flaring.

"How do you feel now with me standing here before you? Feeling brave enough to take me? Or will you prove that you're the pathetic coward you really are, hiding behind your desk, dishing out orders and spreading evil?"

He roared, anger escaping like a geyser, and lunged at her. He aimed a high arcing blow, which Till deflected, but it carried more power than she anticipated. His follow-up attack was quicker than she judged, too, and it forced her back a couple paces. But all her life, she had practised against opponents bigger and stronger than her. Till's talent with a blade lay in her speed and her cunning. She let him think he had the upper hand, and that encouraged him to go for it, to aim a heavy overhand blow at her head. Till ducked, and while crouched down, pounced with her two blades. She sliced the insides of both of his thighs, close to his groin.

The pain didn't hit him right away, but when it did, it took his breath and sent him staggering backwards. He steadied himself against the wall, but she could tell from his unfocused eyes that his head was swimming from the blood rushing down his legs and onto the parquet floor. The sword fell from his grip.

"You fucking bitch," he said, breath ragged, slipping down the wall to sit on the ground.

Till smiled.

"Not nice to feel blood running down your legs, is it?" She kicked his sword away. "I didn't think you'd be done so soon. That was always one thing about you, I suppose. Never lasted long. Not much to show for, either. But you didn't let it stop you, did it? No thought given to the impact of your need for fast gratification, that it was a person you were hurting and destroying? Or was that what got you going?"

Till's anger flowed through her as she walked over to him. He tried to stand, drew a dagger and swiped it at her. She batted it away, knocked it out of his grasp, and sliced off half his hand. A scream tore from his lungs, and he backed away from her into the corner, making a bloody mess of the lavish furniture and papered walls.

"You mad bitch" was all he said over and over through his wails and weeping. No hint of an apology. No sign of remorse. Still blaming others even as he stared death in the eye. His pathetic screams were grating on her. She pummelled him a couple of times over the back of the head with the butt of one of her swords. She smiled with delight as he grunted and groaned. With him shushed by the blows, she took off his belt and bound his hands with it, just like he'd done to her the time he'd whipped her arse and back bloody. She yanked down his breeches and took out her knife. She grabbed his cock, watching his face, waiting for him to come round, to realise what was about to happen. His eyes steadied, then widened. Before he could scream, she cut it off in one slice. She took the fleshy extremity and shoved it into his mouth, too far in for him to spit it out. He coughed and choked as he writhed about in pain, bleeding, dying.

Till stood, picked up one of her swords.

"We're not quite done yet, dear husband. See, we can never truly be even. Because although I'll be walking out of here alive, I carry the scars of what you've done to me. You've inflicted an open wound that will never heal. So that's what I'm going to do to you."

Unable to protest verbally, he rocked his body and kicked his legs, but he couldn't reach her in time to stop the tip of her sword from sinking into the centre of his chest, just below his neck. In a slow, deep motion, she dragged her blade down, slicing him clean open all the way to his crimson groin. Blood, guts, and more spilt forth. He screamed through the cock in his mouth. Till stepped away, looking down at her work. Her smile had faded. So had the anger. She felt at ease, able to breathe without a vice grip of pain and fear crushing her. In that moment, the bonds fell away. Liberation—the theme of the day. Till breathed deep and took one last look at the man who had tried to destroy everything in her life. She turned and left him to die in pain and isolation.

She found Gerida at the bottom of the stairs.

"I followed the sound of the screaming and guessed it was to do with you. I've never heard a man wail like that before," he said. He had a cut on his sword arm. Blood poured down it, but it didn't look deep.

"Let me bandage that for you," she said, ignoring his comment. She had never told anyone but Dhijs what Vaso had done to her, not even her father—how could she have told him? It would have broken his heart to know the truth. Gerida knew enough to understand that she had a score to settle.

They stepped back onto the street to find it buzzing with people, and with no sign of any guards. Coming from the road opposite were rioters and revolutionaries, some carrying torches, others bits of wood or poles. Many of them seemed more interested in looting than anything else. But it meant one thing—they'd broken through the barricades.

"Till!" a young male voice called. She scanned the crowd, trying to find the source of the voice, and locked eyes with a bright-eyed teen with shaggy hair the shade of russet.

"Wylson sent me," he said between gasps. "He said to tell you we've broken through the two central barricades and are gathering at the square leading up to the keep."

"Excellent work. What's your name?"

"Lim, miss."

"You did well to find me, Lim. Head back to Wylson and let him know the western barricade still stands, last we checked. Tell him to send a group to clear it. And Lim, make sure you keep your nose out of trouble now, hear? I want to see you still breathing when the sun rises tomorrow."

He blushed and nodded, and as quickly as he arrived, he fled into the riotous night.

Gerida and Till tried to redirect as many people as they could to the square for the final push. Most followed, though a few were hellbent on seeing through their own agenda of liberating the rich of their possessions and causing as much damage as possible. These people had lived their lives with the sole of the elite's boot across their throats. To live in such a stressful, conflict-ridden society would send most people insane. And here some of them stood now, off to burn whatever they could as an act of demented retribution. Who could blame them?

The press thickened as they neared the square. Till was buoyed to see many of them were clad in armour and carrying shields and myriad weapons—spears, swords, axes, and maces of the flanged variety. These were veterans of wars past, as well as a few younger soldiers, all of them loyal to General Leo. She wondered where the devious old man was now, whether he was safe. She also wondered about all those who had helped today and where they were—the union man, Zia, and of course Dhijs and the likes of little Mal and the other children who had been her eyes and ears across the city. Everyone who had played their part. Without them, they wouldn't have gotten this far. And now the end was in sight.

They meandered their way through the crowd and found a huddle of officers and the men she had planned this revolution with. Some of them saw her coming and stopped talking. They stood tall and straight and saluted, respect clear in their eyes.

"None of that now, fellas. What's the latest?" she asked.

A man named Bartel spoke up, his grey handlebar moustache wobbling.

"We've cleared the centre and the flanks are in progress. More people are streaming up from the city. Tens of thousands, we've heard. As for the keep, we have not heard from Leo's men within the wall. A purple flag was due to be raised from the south tower window, but it hasn't appeared. We can only assume they've been found and killed. However, we cannot see anyone on the walls. There's a chance our enemy might have given up. Or it could be a trap." His voice carried something of a lisp, which in other circumstances would make him hard to take seriously, but the man spoke sense that was hard to argue with.

"What do you all think?" Till asked the group.

"Trap," they said one by one, bar a final grey-haired man named Polik who looked fit for bed, judging from the weariness in his eyes.

"I'm with you. It's likely a trap, and we can't hold out hope that Leo's men will show. There was always a chance that part of the plan wouldn't come off. Canterbury has eyes and ears everywhere. So, what do we do?" Till said.

"The battering rams are being brought up. With such numbers, we could try an all-out assault," Bartel said.

"We have ladders too," another man said.

"When have you ever seen ladders work?" Polik asked him.

"In Tinsy, back in the Swamp Wars."

"When half the defenders were blind drunk?"

"Easy, guys," Till said. "Ladders aren't ideal, but they're something. It's not like we're swimming in a sea of options here." *Only blood*, she thought.

They debated ideas for a short while longer, but it all came back to the single, obvious answer—charge and overwhelm. There was no other way through. It was agreed that they'd try one attack and see what happened. If that didn't work, they would wait them out, besiege them, and regroup. But that also left the risk of their enemies escaping, and Canterbury and his cronies needed to be held accountable, a point vociferously made by many. This couldn't drag on, either, otherwise they'd run the risk of the military returning.

Orders were distributed to form up into ranks. Even citizens were recruited to fill places, and many of them seemed more than willing. A horn blew—time to advance.

Till moved with Gerida and a couple of other officers in the second bank of soldiers. The first marched twenty paces or so ahead. The synchronised thrum of marching feet had her hair standing on end and brought a smile to her lips that broadened at the thought of Vaso's dead body. This was it; the end was here. Take this door, and the city was theirs.

She saw a flash first, a blinding white spark. More of them followed, like stars exploding. The cobbled stone beneath her rumbled and shook, and then everything before her lit up in a vast wall of fire so bright she had to turn away, its heat searing her like the summer sun. The blast left her hearing nothing but whistles and squeals, but she could feel the vibrations of shouts and screams around her. Till tried to move away from the heat, when something struck the back of her head, and darkness swallowed her whole.

The Magpie

The wind pulled at Mydela's cloak. Its chilling fingers pinched the uncovered skin around her eyes, found gaps in her leather armour and mail, and threatened to loosen her weary grip on the rockface.

The crashing waves below masked the clinks of her pickaxes, but now that the parapets were in sight, she paused after every blow, expecting a curious face to appear from above.

A few more feet to go. She heard the roar of thousands of voices carrying on the wind, men and women together. Mydela could feel their defiance. All was going to plan.

Removing a kingdom's elected leaders was risky. The Guild didn't like to interfere with the sovereignty of nations nor the will of the people; it wasn't their place to dictate how nations ruled. Their job was to keep evil at bay. But when it became clear the Dakyra were behind what was happening here in Pietalos, that position changed. Somehow, they'd managed to root themselves amongst the power structures. And without being detected by the Guild until recently, their evil, corruption and rot had spread through the city, forcing the city's people into a chokehold after years of deliberate decline and degradation.

The wheels of revolution had long been in motion before the Guild became involved. It buoyed Mydela to see people fighting back against the Dakyra and the evil they spread. It was individuals who had made this happen—Tillia, the one they called Shadow, and General Leo in particular. Allies of influence were few, but with the will of the people behind them, it was possible.

Everyone had a part to play—the Guild, too—and that was why Mydela was here, to cut the head off the beast, grab the heart of the corruption, and burn it. The Dakyra were no ordinary foe, as Mydela knew well. For months, she'd been their prisoner, tortured, abused, interrogated, left to hang by her arms for days on end in a lightless, stinking pit filled with rats. She often awakened in the dead of night, thinking she was still there, the scars on her arms and back burning afresh. She'd managed to escape in the end, but they'd hunted her down, sending their huge, bat-like creatures called Nyceri after her. It'd taken a long while to get over that, to feel brave enough to venture out into the field and face the Dakyra again. It was why she'd volunteered for this mission as a way of fighting her fears. Now that she was here, drawing close to her target, the scars across her body itched. An invisible hand grasped her chest, the voice it belonged to telling her she couldn't do it. That she was weak, worthless. But feeling that weakness annoyed her. She slammed the first of her pickaxes into the rock, and then the other, banishing that voice with each blow.

Mydela had a score to settle with the Dakyra; not just for the hurt they'd inflicted upon her, but also upon those she loved and had lost, Syara above all. When she'd made it back to the Guild, she'd learned the Dakyra had killed Syara and scores of others. They'd infiltrated somehow, managed to place someone on the inside, then struck when heads were turned. In another time, today's mission would have been a two- or three-person job. Now, the Guild was thin on the ground, and the Dakyra's incursions were becoming more common, sophisticated, and unpredictable. And worryingly, in this case, more destructive and harder to undo. Mydela feared the balance was tipping, and that meant more people would suffer.

The Dakyra's usual play was to slither their way into positions of power, infect the minds of others, and bend them to their will. And once they were rooted, the cogs of their merciless machine turned at frightening speed. Based on the information that General Leo had provided, the Guild had strong suspicions the Dakyra were at work here in Pietalos.

Leo and the Guild had crossed paths decades before. Contact had been lost, but Leo had found a way to reach out. He'd told them of their plans for revolt and how they needed support. The Guild had agreed after digging into Canterbury a little deeper. Despite the rogue politician's elaborate stories of life before he came to Pietalos, none of them checked out. He'd lied about everything—where he was from, place of birth, family, friends. Nobody had ever heard of him. It was as if he'd one day appeared from thin air. With no history, coupled with his calculating, manipulative and evil approach, the Guild were confident that Canterbury was a Dakyran in disguise, but there was only one way to find out for certain.

After years of building his position, Canterbury had, according to Leo, made a play for full control of the city. He'd brought in his own private army and coerced elected officials into signing over power to him, pitching himself as their saviour in these terrible times of hardship. Canterbury had done this under the guise of the "will of the people," but as Mydela hauled herself atop the parapets, she witnessed the genuine will of the people.

Upon the keep's curtain wall, Mydela had a clearer view of what was happening. Three quarters of the wall backed onto the coast. The final quarter faced the city, the gatehouse in the centre of that stretch of wall. Running down the hill from the Upper Town to Lower Town and the Great River, arteries of fire burned. Huge balls of fire consumed bigger buildings—apartment blocks and factories. They each produced dense, toxic plumes of thick black smoke that rose to hang over the city. If it was daylight, the sun's rays wouldn't be able to penetrate it. The stench of burning hung heavy on the breeze. And that breeze carried the sounds of fighting, of chants of revolution, of shouts of anger and frustration, all flowing toward the keep. Part of Mydela wanted to head in that direction, to help see the gate open, but that wasn't her task. Instead, she set off along the wall, staying low, heading for the nearest tower so she could descend to the keep, which stood at the heart of the broad bailey below.

Mydela had taken no more than a handful of steps when the stone beneath her feet shook. She stumbled to one knee, grabbing a crenel for balance. The air around her was sucked away like she was in a vacuum. Then came a deep, rumbling explosion. The volume grew; the ground shook with more violence. Beyond the gate, a series of fireballs swelled in size, bigger than the tallest apartment blocks and burning with the ferocity of a thousand furnaces. They disappeared into roiling clouds of smoke and dust and rocks. The ringing in Mydela's ears wasn't loud enough to drown out the screams and shouts that had replaced those defiant chants. Upon the walls by the gate, archers stood up and moved into position to shoot, but great plumes of smoke charged toward them, and they ducked back down behind the parapets.

Leo had said nothing about Canterbury having access to weapons this powerful. It meant it had to be the work of the Dakyra. But never had Mydela seen the Dakyra use such destructive force. Their strategies were cunning and sly—poisoning a village's well or setting hellish beasts upon towns and farmsteads.

Mydela descended the spiral stairs two at a time, conscious that the momentum had shifted drastically. Her chance could soon disappear altogether.

She opened the door at the bottom of the tower, peered outside. Seeing the courtyard clear, she crossed it to the keep and fell in amongst the shadows. Mydela had studied the plans of the keep, both the original and the extensions—the towers, the newly built People's

Assembly Hall, the wings for guests, the grand banquet hall, and the offices and chambers used by the city's elected officials. What once had been home to kings and queens was now shared by the kingdom's ruling class and enjoyed in similar opulent fashion. Little had changed, save for more greedy people trying to break each other's fingers so they could sink their own into the pie.

Skirting the wall, her right shoulder against the stone, Mydela came to the door she'd selected as her best chance of sneaking inside. The entrance, used by servants, led into the kitchens and store rooms. Two guards stood outside it, the pair very much off-guard and seemingly unmoved by the mass explosions. One was slumped on his spear, eyes closed; the other was hunkered down, poking his dagger at something in the mud. Mydela unhooked her slingshot from her belt, loaded a ball, and took aim at the crouched guard. Her first shot slammed into his forehead, and he fell back on his arse and went limp. Before his comrade could open his eyes, a ball slammed into his head. They'd both wake in a few hours with sore heads and angry bumps. It wasn't the way of the Magpies to kill those the Dakyra manipulated in their schemes if they could help it. They were victims as much as anyone else.

The chaotic sounds fell away as she stepped into the keep. A candle in a wall sconce illuminated the corridor. Another burned further along. She headed toward it. Mydela's first aim was to find Canterbury, and if there were any other Dakyrans around, she'd deal with them too. Word from Leo was that Canterbury had an office in an old library on the first floor, overlooking the bailey and the city beyond. Reputedly, he'd had the books removed and burned when he first seized control, claiming the history of the kingdom would start afresh under his rule. Leo said he spent most of his time there, so that was the place she judged he'd be.

Mydela followed the route she'd memorised. There were no signs of life, even as she moved up the stone stairwell and onto the first floor. She took a right turn, moving past closed doors made of dark wood. At the end of the passage, she saw the glow of torchlight. The murmur of voices drifted toward her too. Mydela slowed to a stop at the edge of the shadows. The voices became clearer.

"He just said keep patrolling around and not to ignore a thing."

"The man's paranoid, I tell you. Who the fuck is gonna be roaming around these corridors? There's a small army guarding the gate out there."

"He seemed pretty serious when he gave the order."

"I swear, we get the shittiest jobs. Don't pull that face at me, Byor. Remember those two weeks we spent in the pissin' rain at that old lighthouse looking out for Kymer ships? They'd forgotten they sent us in the end."

"Yeah, well, it beats being out there killing the people we're meant to be protecting."

"What would you do if they got in here and tried to kill you?"

The pause was telling. "Like I said, I'm glad I'm not out there."

"Don't dodge the question..." The voices trailed off as they moved along the corridor. With them went the torchlight. Mydela turned down the corridor the guards had just travelled along and slowed when she saw two braziers burning on either side of a large wooden door. Canterbury's office.

Mydela drew a throwing knife. She gripped the iron-ringed door handle, turned it, and pushed it open with her shoulder, just wide enough to slip inside. Crouching, she disappeared into the shadow of a large wooden cabinet, letting the door close behind her with a gentle click. Her heart beat a heavy rhythm in her chest as she listened for a response to her intrusion. Perfect stillness, like an empty room, or someone hoping to trick her into making the first move with that idea in her head. She decided to chance a peek.

An iron chandelier hung from from a vaulted ceiling, its two dozen candles illuminating the rectangular room. Stained-glass windows dominated the wall straight ahead. Many of the panes were smashed, no doubt by the explosions. Men and women she didn't recognise were depicted in beautiful detail on those remaining windows, and through the shattered panes beside them, she saw fire and smoke and heard the hubbub of fighting.

Scores of bookshelves lined the other three walls with rows of wooden stacks filling half the room. Rumours of Canterbury's aversion to books proved true. The shelves and stacks were empty. And so, too, it seemed, was the rest of the room, save for a grand wooden desk and single leather-backed chair, carpeted in multicoloured glass from the broken windows.

Mydela moved toward the desk at a crouch, steps soundless, eyes never still, knife at the ready. Her feet crunched against the glass as she approached the paper-covered desk. The chair was tucked neatly behind it. She checked the desk's drawers and found nothing but more documents, some with maps, drawings, and sketches. None of it stood out to her. There was nothing Dakyran, anyway.

Mydela scanned the room once more, frowning as she did. She was sure he'd be here, observing the battle outside. Mydela looked through a broken window pane. The black smoke had eased but still rose from fires that raged where the explosions had erupted. Archers loosed at will from upon the walls. But to her surprise, she found the gate was open. Marching through it were hundreds of pikemen—Canterbury's eastern mercenaries. They were pushing to subdue the rebellion rather than wait it out. Maybe they knew they couldn't wait. Up here in this keep, they'd be trapped. And in a city of half a million, the numbers were stacked against the Dakyra. The people would regroup and come again and again. This was their chance to seize back control, to break the back of the revolution. Mydela just hoped those on the other side of that wall were prepared—that was, if they'd survived the explosions. Before she could look further, a chilling draft brushed the back of her neck. The hairs on her arms bristled. She sniffed and caught the scent of rotten flesh. Grip tight on the hilt of her throwing knife, she turned.

"I wondered how long it would take for the Magpies to arrive. Flit in through the window, did you?" A laugh, a raspy sound to match a voice deep and cold enough to inflict chill blains.

"It's taken you some time. Years, in fact, and only one of you. You're slowing down. Not many of you left?" That same laugh again. Mydela fought a shudder. She'd faced the Dakyra more times than she could count, but she still got a sinking feeling when in their presence, like a hand gripping her heart and plunging it into icy water. It was a hangover from her captivity that she'd never quite overcome. And Canterbury triggered it. His skeletal fingers clutched a tall staff of black wood, a dark stone secured to the top by a messy assortment of string. He was so pale she could see the blue veins on his bald and bulbous head, though she doubted any warm blood pumped through his body. It was his eyes, above all else, that unsettled her. Where human eyes were white, Canterbury's were black as death, his irises the shade of fire. His thin, putrid-hued lips were curled in a smile, his mouth too large for his face. Those lips did a poor job of hiding the rows of teeth sharpened into jagged points. This was the true form of the Dakyra, and being masters of deception, they did a good job of hiding it.

Canterbury's physical appearance wasn't all that he wielded to unnerve her. The Dakyra oozed a sense of dread and despair, a creeping fear that enveloped your soul. Mydela could feel its chilling tingles crawling across her arms, legs, and back. It moved to her head, icy worms burrowing into her brain. His voice danced around inside her head, hissing words she couldn't make out. The old wounds on her arms flared as if touched by hot pokers. Her body racked in pain, as if Canterbury was tearing open those wounds again, trying to break her, sap her willpower. Mydela fought with everything she had, but weariness began to grip. She wanted to lie down, battled to stop her body moving that way. Like a sadist, he delighted in the effect he had on her, until a bang filled the room. Canterbury broke his gaze to look at the windows, and Mydela's fatigue receded like drain water. More crashes sounded through the broken windows, like heavy blows against wood, and judging from the scowl on Canterbury's face, they weren't anticipated. He turned to face her.

"Tell me this, little bird—what is the reasoning behind you provoking a city into revolution? Are the Magpies that short on numbers?"

"Revolution isn't the word. It's more like liberation. And this wasn't our doing. This was the people within this city rebelling against the crooked, evil system you're forcing them to live by. They're fighting for their futures, against you polluting their waters, tearing down their forests, digging toxic mines that people die in every day; against battling to get food and clean water, to look after what little family they have left, to find somewhere safe to sleep, hoping the smogs don't ruin their lungs or that the water doesn't give them dysentry.

"I'm here for you, Canterbury, to see the job through."

Canterbury's smile waned a little. "How very noble. Were you practising that little speech on the way over here?" The red in his eyes flared. "You seek to bring order to chaos, but what you are advocating and supporting is more chaotic than anything we could have conjured." He gave her a hideously wide smile, one that almost took up the bottom half of his face. "I accept the chaos for what it is and let it control itself. Order forms around it."

"Your ordered chaos is very much rebelling against you, it seems," Mydela said.

"This is what chaos is—the world imploding in on itself. Daily routines forgotten. Currencies void. Morals discarded. This is what *you* have created, the very thing you say you oppose."

"Sometimes fire can only be defeated with fire."

"I suppose there is no issue when *you* contradict yourself, but when others do... revolution. What alternative do you offer these people? What does your future look like for them? Are fishermen the new kings, peasants the new nobles, nobles the farmhands? Whatever follows will descend into a pit of even greater bitterness and destruction."

"You doubt these people that much?" Mydela said, her frown deepening.

"Doubt them? I know who they are. I know how they stab each other in the back, if not with whatever shiv they can find, with their words and their dishonesty. Without even a modicum of control, the city will collapse in on itself like the old, crumbling structure it is."

"That is merely your wish, your desire, your fantasy."

"There's a thin line between fantasy and this city."

Another loud bang sounded from outside; a rush of flames rose into the air. Shouts and screams rang out, cries of defiance loud among them. Mydela imagined slaughter of the worst kind taking place. The time for talk was over.

"Since these are your last moments, answer this—what did you hope to gain here? You put a lot of effort into this one," Mydela said, beginning to circle him with knife raised.

Canterbury's eyes glowed like windows to hell. "The gods need an army for when they return."

"They will never return."

Canterbury laughed, a chuckle at first before becoming hysterics.

"And what then? Kill everyone?" Mydela said over his laughter.

He continued to laugh, a marrow-chilling sound.

"You know why we do what we do. And know this, Magpie—we grow closer every day while the wind carries you further away. Soon the time will come when you cannot stop us, when order will fall and chaos will reign. The wheels are turning too fast for you pathetic birds to stop us." His eyes flared, pulsating with power. The stone that was fixed to his staff sparked to life, a glow that grew brighter and brighter, matching his eyes. Mydela had never seen a Dakyran wield such a weapon, but she knew what it was, and the realisation knocked her sick—magea. Those who knew how to harness it had perished in the Great War. Few books on the art of magea, if any, had survived. All that remained were a handful of relics—enchanted amulets, weapons, and pieces of armour. They were tools the Guild rarely used, for in some cases, the enchantments wore off with use.

Whether Canterbury had found this enchanted staff or somehow someone had made it, didn't matter. The fact was they had it, and it changed things. The sinking feeling in her gut confirmed just how significantly so.

Canterbury broke into more demented laughter as he watched her fear reveal itself. In a burst of movement, he brought up his staff and pointed it at her. Crimson light flashed, blinding her, but she had the sense to move. Blinking, she looked over her shoulder, and through spotted vision, saw a beam of jagged red light smash the stone slabs where she'd stood a moment before. She kept running, fear trying to freeze her legs. Never had she faced such power. *How can I stop it?*

Mydela headed for the nearest stack of bookshelves and ducked down an aisle for cover. She had time for nothing else before splinters exploded beside her. The sizzling beam of red light pulverised the wood and stone floor. Rocks and chippings shotblasted her, and she fled once more. The end of the stack loomed, and she braced herself to emerge from cover, her throwing knife tight in her grip. The beam of magea pursued. She broke free of the wooden shelves, slid along the ground, and sent her blade spinning in Canterbury's direction.

The Dakyran turned his staff on her without hesitation, sending that searing beam right at her. But it faltered and died. The blade sunk into his abdomen, between chest and gut. Canterbury hissed with pain and rage and spoke words in the archaic Dakyran language that Mydela understood little of. He pulled the knife slowly free of his body and dropped it on the ground, black blood covering the area around it.

"The bird likes to peck."

He slammed the butt of his staff against the ground, and light exploded from the crystal. Mydela headed for cover. She heard wood shattering, stone breaking, but her legs kept moving, and she felt no pain. Soon, she found herself behind another stack. The lights flashing in her eyes faded, and she could see the violent sparks of light reflecting on the walls. Canterbury was directing his attacks at the other side of the room. He must have blinded himself, too, and lost sight of her. A chance.

Mydela drew another couple of throwing knives. She needed to get close to the bastard if she was to end this. Besides, she was running out of hiding spots.

Mydela crept to the end of the stack, peered around the edge. Canterbury dragged the beam around the room, splintering wood and breaking stone and cleaving deep gouges in the floor. She was just out of his eyeline; if he turned, she'd be done for. So she moved low and fast, soundless like a shadow, and further out of his line of view. Her gaze remained on the Dakyran, his back to her. Thirty paces away, she let rip with her first knife, throwing everything into it. She sprinted after it, pausing about fifteen paces away to hurl her second knife. The first blade plunged into his back, the second a few inches above it. She drew her shortsword, lifted it high as she neared the lanky figure, and swung.

She cut air.

Canterbury ducked low, spun, and swung his staff to bludgeon her back. Mydela staggered forward but stopped herself from falling. Grimacing but angered by the pain, she turned and arced her sword at his neck. The Dakyran brought up his staff and parried, the wood hard as steel. He laughed and licked his thin lips. Mydela kicked at the stomach wound she'd inflicted earlier. It broke their stalemate, but he didn't react in the way she'd hoped. He took a few steps back as if unphased, and the crystal affixed to his staff began to pulsate. Mydela leapt at him, desperate to stop it. The blow aimed at his neck forced him to bring up his staff, and the light faded.

Sweat ran down her brow and back. Her sword arm tingled from the clashes against Canterbury's staff. But her pace and ferocity grew. This was her one chance at taking him; to fail here would see her end, and maybe the end of everyone fighting in the city. That thought spurred her on even more. Her legs moved with an extra spring; the fatigue in her arms melted away. She attacked again, this time feinting a blow and sliding it down the staff. With a flick of her wrist, she took a chunk out of his shin.

That sent him back a few paces. He hopped, leapt, and ran away from her. Mydela chased him down, lost her footing on a pothole blasted into the stone. She smashed her knee against the ground as she fell. Pain exploded. She looked up and found the red light glowing, a smile upon Canterbury's face. The beam hurtled toward her.

Mydela did all she could to pick herself up, to get out of the way, scratching and clawing and kicking the ground. Heat seared her shoulder, a glancing blow, but enough to send her back to the ground. She hit her knee again as she fell and the agony that erupted kept her conscious.

Gritting her teeth against the pain, she willed herself to her feet as the beam came after her again. She threw herself out of the way, landing on her side, and yanked a dagger out of her boot. Canterbury aimed the staff at her.

She sent her knife spinning. It sunk, hilt-deep, into his right eye. Canterbury dropped to the ground. The staff rattled against the stone, and the light in the crystal died.

Mydela dropped to her arse and lay back, gasping for air, fighting the throbbing soreness consuming her shoulder, arm, and knee. She glanced down at the wound and saw nothing but raw redness at the top of her shoulder stretching down to her chest—no leather armour, no skin. She wouldn't be surprised if it had burned everything away down to muscle and bone. The thought sent a wave of bile up from her gut. She spewed it out. This morning's breakfast, and something else with it. Streaks of black that twisted like worms in the bilious mulch. She couldn't think about it now and what it meant. The job wasn't done, and nothing else mattered until then.

With pain growing in her knee, which she was sure she'd either dislocated or fractured, she hobbled over to Canterbury's prone form, using her sword as a walking aid. Black blood pooled around his head. From her belt, she took out the small skin of Namas Oil—a fuel that burned with such fierce heat it turned bodies to ash in minutes. It was the only way they could ensure the complete extermination of a Dakyran and the evil within them. She doused his body with it, covering every inch—the merest drop would burn with frightening intensity. She sparked a match, and Canterbury's body erupted in flames, sizzling, crackling. How many people had died, on both sides, because of this bastard? Everyone who Canterbury wooed to his cause was just as much a victim as those fighting against it out in the city; many of them didn't realise it.

The door clicked open behind her. Mydela turned, lifting her sword. She found a woman, face covered in soot, grime, and blood, her long black hair mostly fallen out of its ponytail and stuck to her sweaty face in strands. She wore black leather armour, not dissimilar to the Magpies' own attire, and she had more than a few cuts and gashes on her arms. Despite it all, Mydela couldn't help but marvel at the perfect shape of her face and her large, striking green eyes. It was enough to catch her breath; not many women had done that in her time, and none since Syara.

"Who are you?" the woman asked.

"My name is Mydela. You must be Tillia."

"How do you know my name?" Her voice was firm, just like the grip on her two swords, but she swayed where she stood.

"It's a pretty long story, but the short answer is General Leo."

Tillia frowned. "You still haven't answered my question."

"My name is Mydela." It wasn't commonplace for the Magpies to tell people who they were and what they did, but Mydela was in too much pain and time was too short to beat around the bush.

"You'll learn more about this soon, but I'm from a group whose job is to stop people like Canterbury." She pointed to the sizzling fire beside her. "He wasn't what he seemed. He was Dakyran. They're an ancient race of pure evil. They corrupt, manipulate, and scheme their way into positions of power and then bend people to their will, all for one purpose—to return their masters to their seat of power.

"Their masters happen to be evil gods, and the Dakyra would do anything if it meant taking a step closer to summoning them to Tervia. It's their sole purpose, the reason for their creation a thousand years ago. They forever search for the means to open portals to the realm of the gods. It's what happened a millenium ago, and it led to the destruction of much of civilization in a war that nobody won.

"When the Dakyra were created, the forces of good forged the Guild, a secretive order serving Udira, Goddess of Balance, arbiter of the struggle between the Light and the Nothingness. Our aim is to quell the Dakyra when they rise up, if not to extinguish their dark light altogether—if such a thing is possible."

"What's been happening here has been going on for a decade. If your job is to track these people down, what happened? Where have you been?"

"That is something we need to get to the bottom of. No Dakyran has ever achieved something like this. And do not think that they will not return. They will. And soon. Evil is like the tide. It may retreat, but it's always there, inching closer.

"Leo spoke highly of you, Tillia. In fact, he said without you, none of this would have been possible. 'A fantasy' were his words. But now the true challenge comes—rebuilding not just a broken city but a fractured society. The Dakyra conquer by division. That was why Canterbury waged war against the poor and afflicted, turning the streets into a daily fight for survival. His kind seek to create a system of chaos and then call it order. It's up to people like you to try and mend those rifts. I do not envy the challenge, but Leo said he had no doubt you can do it." A wave of light-headedness struck Mydela. She wobbled on her feet and put much of her weight on her sword. She breathed deep, head swaying.

"You speak as if I am now in charge of this city," Tillia said.

Mydela breathed deep, and her head began to clear. "Who else, Tillia? Who led this revolution? Who stood up for the people when no one else would? Who fought for them, inspired them, instilled them with hope? You have led some of them through the greatest battle in all of their lives. You are their natural leader. But the battle is over now. These people need stability and guidance. And above all, you need to make sure that whatever political order comes next, the Dakyra cannot infiltrate it."

Tillia lowered her swords, her blood-stained hands loosening on the hilts. The fierce look in her eyes began to melt, and through the cracks, Mydela saw uncertainty.

"Good people have helped you achieve this today. Keep them close. The Magpies will be close too."

"Magpies?"

Mydela pulled the iron brooch pinned to the lapel of her cloak—a silhouette of a magpie, not much bigger than a fingertip. The long tail was smooth from her stroking it, something she often did when she had things on her mind. She approached Tillia and handed it to her. "It is the moniker of the Guild. A white and black bird to represent the balance between Life and the Nothingness."

Shouts rang out along the corridor outside Canterbury's office. Mydela had to move. Not only did she have to get back as soon as possible to warn the others what she'd found, but the Guild had to remain a secret, out of the public eye. Too many questions would get asked by too many people if they saw her now, and gossip would spread like the plague. It would be devastating for the effectiveness of the Guild's work if word got out—a population of non-believers who didn't understand the reality of the world would grow suspicious and cynical, and the Dakyra would prey on that weakness, using it to sway public opinion against the Magpies. But Mydela wasn't quite sure her knee would allow her that chance to escape, and her shoulder burned like fire. She looked at Tillia.

"Can you help me out of here?"

Tillia looked over her shoulder at the half-open door. She pushed it closed and dropped the small iron bar to lock it. She turned and looked at Mydela, eyes giving nothing away. Mydela's fingers wrapped around the hilt of her sword.

"There's a hidden door over there," Tillia said, pointing. "Let me help you." She held out an arm. Mydela hesitated for a moment but accepted and shifted her weight off her sore knee and onto Tillia.

"Thank you, Tillia. I will not forget this, and nor will the Guild."

They took a few steps toward the east wall before she stopped. "Wait," Mydela said. With a bit of effort, she bent down and picked up Canterbury's staff. The crystal was still attached, though it was now a deep, crimson colour and devoid of any light. The smooth wood was cold as rock and weighed as little as a quill. If she could get it back to the Guild, maybe someone could figure out whether it was a relic or something the Dakyra had made. She sheathed her sword and used the staff to support her.

"My hus—ex-husband, now deceased, had the plans for the keep in his office, so I took them," Tillia said as she kicked a few stones in the wall with the flat of her foot. At last, one clicked, and a door, hidden among the stone, popped open. They ducked inside and closed the door behind them. It was black as a Dakyran's heart, so Mydela took out her light crystal from the pouch hanging on her belt. The white glow of the crystal began to beat away the gloom.

"What on Tervia is that?" Tillia asked, eyes wide.

"It's a special type of crystal that can capture light and reflect it. A woman much wiser than I said it's like an endless hall of looking glasses that the light bounces against. It gets trapped in there."

Tillia gave her an appreciative nod.

"I need to get to the cellars beneath the kitchen quarter. There's a tunnel that'll take me down to the coast. I have a boat there."

"Are you sure you can make that? You can barely stand, let alone row a boat. And what about your arm? I'm not gonna lie; it looks nasty."

Mydela didn't want to think about it. "Tell me, what happened at the gate? I saw the explosions. Was that you or them?"

"Them. We were about to charge when they went off. I got knocked out and woke up under bodies and rocks. Be damned if I know how I'm still alive. So many didn't make it." A grimness gripped her voice. "Then the bastards appeared through the smoke with their pikes and shields and started butchering us. But there were only a few thousand of them, and the people came like a tsunami and washed them away. With all the smoke, they couldn't see us coming on the wall, and before they realised, we were flooding through the gate." A smile that oozed pride had fixed itself on her face.

Mydela smiled, but a fresh wave of agony gripped her. Vomit lurched from her gut, a thick black substance that burned her throat. It stunk of rot and glistened in the light of the crystal. Again, it looked like it was moving. Sweat ran down her brow, more from the panic of what was happening to her than the pain. But the nausea eased, and with Tillia's help, she got to her feet.

They went on, and Mydela found a rhythm that kept her aches to a minimum. Her arm continued to sting and burn, but there wasn't much she could do about that until she got back to the boat and her travel pack of supplies. She had plenty of aloe and tinctures that would fix her up. But one thing she wasn't sure about was the magea's lasting impact. Some weapons carried enchantments that inflicted poison-like effects. If there was a cure for those, no one knew what it was. Mydela shoved those thoughts out of her mind as more shouting sounded through the walls.

"Do you think you can manage a ladder?" Tillia asked.

"If I must, then yes."

They soon arrived at the end of the narrow passageway and came to a set of ladders side by side—one heading up, another heading down. Mydela sized up the one heading down. It didn't have too many rungs, but bending her knee that many times would be a big ask. "If you climb down first, do you think you can break my fall if I slide down?"

Tillia looked her up and down and nodded.

"Let's try it."

Tillia disappeared, and then it was Mydela's turn to line herself up for her descent. She'd done this plenty of times, just never with a fucked shoulder and knee. She shouted down to Tillia, then dropped, doing her best to control her speed with her palms. Before she came close to hitting the ground, firm hands grabbed her back and arse and lowered her.

Mydela nodded her thanks, and with an arm around Tillia once more, they set off. The celebrations seemed to fill the keep now. More than a few glasses and pots smashed while people sung and cheered.

The time came to leave the secret passageways. Tillia was skilled at dancing between the shadows, an instinctive grace that Mydela couldn't help but admire. Soon enough, they were in the kitchens. No revolutionaries had found it yet, but no doubt it would be ransacked within the hour. Tillia helped her into the cellar, and after shifting a few barrels, they found a long-forgotten hatch with an iron bar across it. Tillia forced it open with a bit of effort.

"So that's the reason I couldn't come in this way," Mydela said.

Tillia hefted open the hatch. "This one wasn't on my map. I'll have to remember it in case the people ever revolt against me."

Mydela managed a smile. "They won't, I'm sure." She broke into a fit of coughing and battled to stop herself from throwing up again. After some deep breaths, the urge passed.

"Why not rest here, out of sight? I can get you what you need."

"No, I must warn the others. Things have... changed. Please, Tillia, make no mention of our meeting, nor anything I've told you. We will return and answer all of your questions. Until then, stay true to yourself. Do not give in to the pain in your heart. Do not let it taint your thinking."

Tillia's eyes glistened. "It will stay between us alone."

Mydela, fighting the pain in her knee, lowered herself into the tunnel. She looked back at Tillia, at her deep green eyes, at the cuts and bruises, the cracked lip.

"Remember today, Tillia. The day the people rose up against evil and won. You will need to remember this strength when it returns."

A Few Weeks Later...

"Thought I'd find you down here."

Till smiled and looked up at Dhijs. His bald head with its curly wisps of white at the sides blocked out the sun. A broad grin was fixed on his face.

"You're a creature of habit, though you've done a good job of destroying most of your old routines," he said, sitting down on the wall beside her.

"Not quite," Till said. He knew her too well. What better adviser to have at her side?

The docks bustled with life once more. The clean-up in the days after the revolution had been long and arduous, but the people got behind her and the new order that was forming. The aim was to create stability, a foundation upon which to build, and the building had begun in earnest. At every turn, she reminded the people that they were building the life they wanted, not the life they were forced to accept.

Once funerals had taken place, the streets cleared of debris, burned buildings demolished and cleared, life began to sprout like seedlings out of soil freshly tilled. Hawkers returned to the streets and squares to sell food and goods. The bay was being dredged and trade ships were beginning to return. Carts laden with supplies clogged the streets and squares. Workers returned to the factories and fields, only this time, they owned a stake in the company. And in Tewbrucke and other parts of Low Town, the streets were free of pushers, thieves, and muggers. In their place, laughing children played games—hide and seek, tag, guards and robbers. The veteran soldiers, volunteers from the uprising, and city guards who had defected now made up the city's policing force, and they had done a stellar job so far, helping people where they could and keeping general order—no looting, no fighting, no murder. It was the calm after the storm, and Till found it a metropolitan utopia.

"Busy morning?" she asked.

"Just the usual. There are always broken fingers to straighten, cuts to stitch."

"We thought life would never be the same again. We sat in this very spot when we said it."

Dhijs laughed. "In many ways, it's different. Better."

"Definitely better. The streets are much safer, for one." Making the decision to go after other bad eggs in the city had been a tough one. But with the muscle they had mustered, it had been more than possible. And after over a year of stalking, tracking, and hitting the crime lords, gangs, and pushers in the city, she knew it was necessary. They had no moral compass, no code to live by. The depraved acts she saw them commit had been too numerous to count—the rapes and sexual assaults, the unprovoked stabbings, beatings, murders. These people were a law unto themselves; indeed, they had no law overseeing them. The corrupt guards, led by her now-dead husband, had been as complicit in it all as anyone. But now it felt like the city could breathe. People could leave their homes without fear. And here they were, sweeping out the dust of a decade of moral chaos, mending fences, doors, windows. Helping their neighbours. That confidence had restored their pride, their humanity. And Till was determined to see it stay that way.

A new political system was being planned; a new constitution drawn up too. Mydela the Magpie's words had stuck with her—to make sure nobody like Canterbury could ever worm their way in again. It would be tough, but it was perhaps the most important thing of all. Till had spent many a long night thinking about solutions to the problem, and in the end, had resolved to copy the Magpies—to create a group devoted to finding and uprooting the evil of the Dakyra. Gerida was helping her with that, ably as always. He'd sustained a nasty cut to his shoulder blade in the final battle when the mercenaries working for the Dakyra left the safety of the keep to crush the rebellion. Gerida had fought like a demon; they all had. Once the people saw those doors open, it had rallied every attacker who had survived that soul-shaking explosion. With sheer numbers, they had bowled through the spears and shields.

"What news of the election?" Dhijs asked, breaking her focus on the shimmering water of the bay.

"None as yet. The constitution is still being decided, but I hear Zia is running for office."

Dhijs clapped his hands, smiling. "Excellent. And there's still no chance of a return to a single leader?"

Till scoffed.

"There's a lot to be said for having a single person in charge, Till, a person like you who the people love, who they can get behind and trust. Someone who'll do the right thing by them."

"You'd have more luck seeing a wildman from the northern mountains than finding an honest man in this city."

Dhijs laughed. "True. It will take time to instil a new culture and inspire a different way of thinking."

"Nonetheless, the time of kings and queens is over," Till said. "It's a daft system, when you think about it. Hundreds of years ago, some violent bastard kills a few people, and through might alone, claims dominion over the land. Once he dies, his spoiled, out-of-touch kids take over, and it carries on like that; there's absolutely no right for those people to rule over everyone else."

"You don't have to remind me; I was part of the first uprising against King Hidalgh. We thought we were doing right when we set up the People's Assembly, but look at what happened."

"Parliament is a good idea, but it should be a house made of glass. Those who sit inside must serve the people they represent and must be accountable for their actions. It shouldn't be a way of gaining power or using it to make yourself rich. The system is broken and needs fixing."

"Well, there are plenty of willing hands to help you."

"I'm still trying to get the hang of the art of delegation."

"Do not fear that someone might fail. Trust that they'll succeed, just as you trusted them before. Remember your own words, Till: 'Together we rise.'"

Till laughed, but it was cut short by pain. Her arm was in a sling, more than a few gashes in the process of healing. She'd broken a few ribs, too, and had a deep cut that was also healing up the side of her lower leg. Dhijs was right, though. These last few weeks had shown her that others were around and able to help rebuild this city, this civilization. And she had to trust them, as hard as it was. She'd trusted them before, so she could and would do so again, from Little Mal and Zia the union man, to people like General Leo and his proud veterans.

"Have you heard any more from the Magpies?" Dhijs asked her, his mirth fading.

She looked at him before her gaze switched to the Great River's slow-moving waters. She'd decided to tell Dhijs, but him alone. She needed his advice on the things she'd heard.

"No, not yet."

"At least we know we have someone looking out for us." Dhijs grumbled as he rose to his feet. He took in the scene around them: the groups of dockers standing round, smoking, laughing, joking; the fisherwomen selling the catch of the day and chatting with others; the children chasing each other around.

"It definitely feels better," he said. "But seeing the frown on your face, I'd almost dare to say you don't agree."

"It's not that. Just something Mydela said stuck with me. Remember, she had to get back and warn the others. She didn't say why, but afterwards, I looked in Canterbury's emptied library and took in the destruction in there. I dread to think what she had to deal with. If that would have been me fighting Canterbury, would I have come out alive?" She sighed. "I keep thinking about the last words she said to me, and ever since, I've not been able to shake this feeling that something bad is coming, like we've woken a beast that longs for our blood."

Dhijs put a reassuring hand on her shoulder. "It is a worry for tomorrow. We have yearned too long for today. You have helped change the lives of tens of thousands of people, Till, all for the better. They have futures, reasons to hope again. *You* have done that. Enjoy it. And when the darkness does return, we'll stand and face it together."

Read More On Patreon

If you enjoyed this story, you'll be pleased to learn that this is but a drop in the ocean. I'm forever writing stories set in my fantasy world of Tervia, as well as more literary pieces that explore a range of issues, from homelessness to Nigel Farage's divisive rhetoric.

You can access all stories, plus new ones that are released each month, on my Patreon page. For the price of a cup of coffee (in fact less than that with inflation) you can read dozens of fantasy and literary stories, plus my debut fantasy novel, Pariah's Lament.

You can also access audio versions of stories, find character art and concept artwork, and uncover the stories behind the stories.

To join today, simply scan the QR code below.

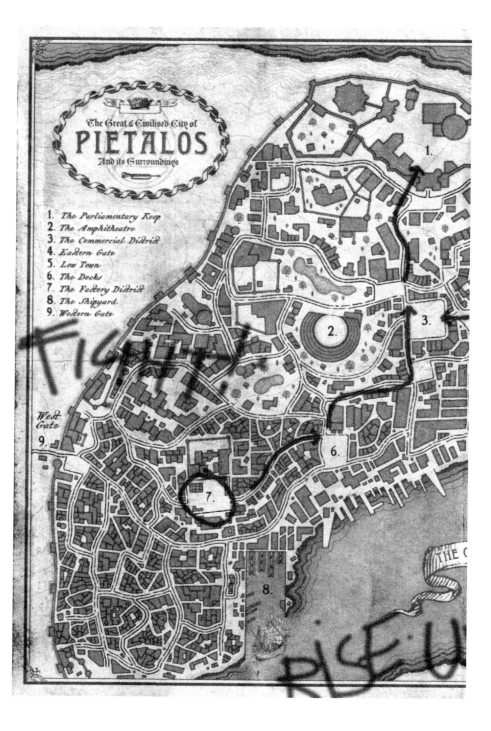

The Great & Civilised City of
PIETALOS
And its Surroundings

1. The Parliamentary Keep
2. The Amphitheatre
3. The Commercial District
4. Eastern Gate
5. Low Town
6. The Docks
7. The Factory District
8. The Shipyard
9. Western Gate

West Gate
9.

THE C

Author's Note

On the day I finished editing this book, Donald Trump was elected to his second term as president, running on the back of a campaign based on policies of anti-immigration and anti-women's rights, policies that are designed to divide us as people and, in our fractured state, make us easier to control.

These choices are driven by a system that I have come to loathe: capitalism. We're born into it, become ensnared in it, and live our lives perpetuating the problems it creates.

Being from a working-class background and living in that environment, you see the harsh realities on a daily basis. You come to accept that it is what it is—a fact echoed in this story. But there comes a point when the cold light of day penetrates through, and you ask yourself, is this really all there is? Is this all we get for the rest of our lives? Is this our very purpose?

To walk around asking existential questions like these is enough to drive you to madness. But there comes a time when we do ask, and we wonder, and maybe, we act.

This book is about the *maybe*. The grand "what if". "What if" we decided that capitalism wasn't for us? What if we decided it had pushed us too far with its unfairness, its injustices, its cold, callous ways? It's not something we think about often, and it's hard to imagine what a different world would feel like. But in a world so devoid of hope, we need to feel some kind of power, some kind of control over our own lives and destinies. Once we feel the warmth that spark of hope offers, we can stoke those flames into belief, and then into a furnace of action. And maybe someday, the world will be a better, fairer place.

Richie

Acknowledgements

Writing a book is a group effort and I'm grateful to everyone who has helped and supported me throughout the process. I'd like to thank Stuart Bache for creating a brilliant and fitting cover, and Jack Shepherd for giving incredible artistic life to the city of Pietalos in the form of the map.

I'd also like to thank my editor, Jennia D'Lima, for her patience and advice. And big thanks go to my partner, Jess, for her enthusiastic encouragement and support, and my mum, Angela, for always being there to give sage advice.

Above all, I'd like to thank you for taking a chance on this book. I sincerely hope you enjoyed it.

About The Author

Richie Billing writes all kinds of stories, but mostly fantasy fiction. His tales often explore real-world issues in unfamiliar settings, zooming in on the characters and their troubles. His short fiction has been widely published, with one story adapted for BBC radio.

His debut novel, *Pariah's Lament*, was published by Of Metal and Magic Publishing in March 2021.

Richie also hosts the podcast **The Fantasy Writers' Toolshed**, a venture inspired by his acclaimed craft book, *A Fantasy Writers' Handbook*.

When not writing, Richie works as an editor and digital marketer and teaches creative writing both online and in his home city of Liverpool. Most nights you can find him up into the early hours scribbling away or watching the NBA. Find out more at www.richiebilling.com.

Printed in Great Britain
by Amazon

59425529R00086